MISTLETOE, MOCHA, AND MURDER

AN ORCHARD HOLLOW NOVELLA

A.N. SAGE

OLIVERHEBERBOOKS

Mistletoe, Mocha, and Murder Copyright 2024 © by A. N. sage

Cover Art by Cauldron Press

Published by Oliver-Heber Books

0 9 8 7 6 5 4 3 2 1

CONTENTS

CHAPTER 1

The smell of burned gingerbread wafted through the air, followed by the intermittent sound of a blaring fire alarm. My arm ached from beating down the smoking, charred remains of the saddest cookie house to have ever existed. In the living room, across from me in the kitchen, my mother balanced on a wooden stool and batted a wet tea towel at the shrieking round box on the ceiling. Her foot lost balance and my eyes rounded in horror as Mom slipped off the stool. Not losing momentum, she waved a hand, muttered a few words and her magic swirled over the chair at her feet. It righted instantly, leaving my mother unharmed.

"That sound is going to drive me mad!" she

shrieked, slapping the fire alarm so hard it stopped ringing. An invisible string pulled at the edges of her lips and she turned to me, proud as a peacock. A second later, the fire alarm resumed its incessant screams. "Darn it! Piper, do something. Please."

I looked from her to the burned dessert I was battling on the counter. "Trying to."

As we continued to get a chokehold on our respective situations, I couldn't help but chuckle. Two witches living under one roof was not ideal, especially when they were as opposite as Mom and me. Ever since Gran died and my wayward creator came back into the picture, I had been struggling with finding my own place at the farmhouse. After all, I did pretty well building a life all on my own. But then moments such as today happened, and it all clicked.

Mom was a wild card, and that was exactly what I needed in my life.

I glanced at the blackened gingerbread pieces. Even if she did come with a side of fire.

Tossing our attempt at decorating into the trash, I picked up the broom sitting by the front door and walked into the living room. Standing directly under the fire alarm, I waved that thing around like my life depended on it, hoping that the wind it created would make the noise subside. If it was possible, it somehow made the alarm even louder.

An exasperated groan sounded from the stair landing, drawing my attention away from the task at hand. Standing there with her arms folded over her transparent chest and an expression of sheer boredom on her face was none other than Stella Rutherford. The ghost, who also happened to be my familiar, rolled her eyes and sauntered toward us. "Step aside."

I tugged at Mom's sleeve and helped her down off the stool before she collided with the spirit. Having been tethered to Stella because of my special magic— thank you, Father Hades—had taught me that getting slammed by spirit energy was about as fun as getting drop-kicked by a linebacker. It was cold, heart-stopping, and sometimes slimy. Zero out of ten, would not recommend.

Since Mom couldn't see Stella like I did, she obeyed instantly, giving the ghost a wide berth.

I watched as the ghost floated up to the fire alarm, cracked her slender, manicured fingers and shoved them into the box. There was a spark and a crackle before the alarm shut down for good. Coming back down, Stella's self-assured face beamed with pride. "You're welcome."

"Thanks, Stella," I said. "Good thing you were here."

Another thing I learned from years of being

friends with the snobby, rich dead woman was that compliments were Stella's favorite currency.

"Very lucky for you, indeed," the ghost replied. "Why are you two setting the house on fire a few days before Christmas?"

I laughed, pointing to the crispy baking sheet with a soot outline of what used to be a gingerbread house wall on it. "Mom wanted to make fun decor for the dinner we're hosting."

"The local coven would have loved the houses," my mother said. She brushed invisible lint from her long knitted skirt and stalked back to the kitchen. "I planned on decorating them to match all their homes. We should try again."

"Please let Sylvie know I don't have it in me to be fighting with fire alarms all day," Stella retorted.

I shook my head, pulling the stool back to the front entrance. "Big plans for your afterlife, huh?"

The remark earned me a stuck-out tongue followed by a less innocent gesture. When Stella finished mocking me, she looked around the farmhouse, her brows slanting in concern. Checking a few corners and under the couch, she vanished from sight, only to reappear at the foot of the stairs again.

"Looking for someone?" I asked.

"Where's the beast?"

My gaze flicked from her to the front door, then

back again. It had been some time since I'd seen Harry Houdini. Last I recalled, the raccoon was digging in the front yard and I had to chase him away before he made a hole deep enough for someone to fall into. The thing about living in a town that swam with paranormal beings was that even the animals acted strange. Harry, the raccoon I had somehow managed to adopt, was no exception. The rascal was always getting into trouble, which added another level of stress to my already chaotic life. I was convinced the ley lines that fueled all our magic got to him as well.

I couldn't prove it, but Mom said it was a good theory, so I ran with it.

"I haven't seen him in a bit," I told Stella. "Maybe he hitched a ride with the mailman back into town."

The ghost's grin widened. "Or out of town. Which would be preferable."

I waved her off.

"You know you love the furball. Don't even pretend otherwise," I teased. "Now come help me find the Christmas lights in the attic. I want to string them up before the sun goes down."

"Let's make a pit stop at the bathroom so you can brush your hair first."

Shaking my head, I started for the second floor when the loud ringing over my head made me stand stock still. Above me, the fire alarm had started up again and as I turned to Mom in the kitchen, my eyes watered. Smoke rose all around us, a heavy base that made my nose wiggle and itch. I watched with narrow eyes as Mom lifted a second tray of burnt gingerbread cookies from the oven, guilt coating her face.

She shrugged. "Baking was definitely more your Gran's specialty than mine."

Exchanging twin looks of worry, Stella and I sucked in sharp breaths and got to work. I ran for a towel while she floated up to the ceiling to deal with the alarm, Mom hot on my heels with the broom. Between the three of us, we had the holidays handled. I looked at the hot mess that was the farmhouse.

If we managed to keep the place from burning to the ground first.

CHAPTER 2

Mugs and empty plates with crumbs on them filled the tables of Bean Me Up to the brim. My eyes flitted to the spaceship-shaped clock above the door with little alien arms marking the time. Half-past three.

I wiped my brow and removed my espresso stained apron, tossing it on the back of a nearby chair. The afternoon rush was officially over.

It had been over a year since I opened the cafe on Cliff Row, our town's most prominent landmark street, and I was finally getting the hang of running it. There were a few hiccups along the way, most involving dead bodies, unfortunately, but things have really settled down lately. Hiring Rory, a young local witch, to help out had a lot to do with it, though even without her aid, I somehow found my groove as a business owner. And now that Rory had left for holiday break with her family, I had to pull up the gloves and do the bulk of the work myself. Mom helped out here and there, but she was still learning the ropes of the business, though her people skills were far superior than mine. I couldn't say the same for her coffee making abilities.

My fingers twitched and blue sparks of electricity covered my skin, zapping at random objects. I grimaced, shoving my hands into the pockets of my cardigan before the few customers still sitting saw. Now, if I could only get a grip on the magic I inherited from my father, Lord of the Underworld.

Biting my tongue, I waited until the magic resolved itself and settled back into my body before clearing out the tables and wiping them down. Just because Orchard Hollow was a bustling center for all things paranormal didn't mean I had to announce the existence of magic to humans. That would be uncouth.

I sprayed down the tabletops, waiting until I could no longer feel the familiar roll of my stomach to move on. As I stood up straight, the welcome doorbell rang out behind me. I spun on my heels, my mood instantly brightening.

"Joe! Hi!" I exclaimed, rushing to greet my

boyfriend at the door. "What brings you by? Everything all right at the bookstore?"

The vampire leaned down to give me a quick peck on the cheek, the smell of peppermint filling my nostrils. "All good. I closed down early, so I figured I'd pop in to see how you're doing."

"You missed the rush," I said, gesturing to the yet to be turned down tables. "But I survived. Want a drink to hold?"

Since vampires couldn't eat or drink human food, there was no point offering, but I knew Joe liked to keep up appearances. Whenever we went out for dinner, he ordered a full meal, never eating any of it. Which was completely fine by me since I got to save whatever deliciousness he left behind. I looked over my shoulder. A fifth coffee wouldn't be heavenly to round out my day. I had recently added an Eggnog Cappuccino to the menu, and it was quickly becoming a favorite of mine.

Rushing to finish cleaning up the tables, I loaded the dishwasher and got to work. The espresso machine hissed to life; I relaxed at the sound of coffee beans grinding in the top canister. Very few things brought me pure pleasure and coffee was always one of them.

I glanced at Joe, leaning against the wall next to me. And him, of course.

When I was done, I slid the steaming mug onto a

tray and gestured to an open table. "Before I forget," I said, sitting down across from Joe. "Mom wanted to make sure you're still bringing your friend to dinner." My voice lowered to a mere whisper. "The werewolf."

"Actually, Brian is why I'm here today."

Oh, no. Please don't let him cancel on me. I would not hear the end of it if the dinner my mother meticulously planned for weeks was going off the rails.

"Is he unable to make it?" I asked, trying to hide the whimper in my voice.

Joe swirled a spoon in the foam of his drink, his green eyes never leaving my face. "Definitely. Brian wouldn't miss it, especially with Lisa taking the girls out of town to her parent'place for the holidays."

"How come he's not going with them?"

"He said he's meeting them for New Year's," Joe explained. "Has some loose ends to tie up for his private investigation firm."

Checking to see that no one was looking, Joe pushed the drink my way, waiting until after I took a sip to slide it back to his side of the table. It was a routine we had become quite used to. For two paranormals that wouldn't normally date, we did well enough to make our differences work.

"Anyway, Brian has a friend in the city who's an established art collector and he invited us for a big fancy opening the guy is throwing. Apparently, it's the most anticipated art opening King City has seen in years." Joe rolled his shoulders, making them appear ever wider under his cowl neck sweater. "Would you want to go?"

I winced. "Eek. I'm not sure. Mom is really excited about this dinner."

"That's the best part!" Joe exclaimed. "We'll be back long before the dinner. What do you say?"

In my chest, my heart galloped with excitement. The last time we visited King City was to follow a lead in a case I had no business interfering with. And with all the work Mom had been making me do for the dinner, I certainly enjoyed the idea of a break. My eyes glimmered. "Well, then, why not? It sounds like it will be fun!"

"And relaxing," Joe added.

"And that," I agreed.

I was about to steal another sip of Eggnog Cappuccino when the door to the back office flew open and the slicing shuffle of tiny paws filled the cafe. My head spun to the door, then a few feet over where Harry Houdini skidded across the tile in a mad dash. Raccoon drool marked his jaw and his cheeks were puffed out, four giant chocolate chip cookies sticking out of it.

Groaning, I stood up, my head instantly pounding with irritation. I looked at the two customers and their shocked faces. My hands shot up in surrender and I nudged my head toward the office so Joe could grab the broom I used to herd the trash bandit outside.

"Nothing to worry about, folks," I told the customers. "Simply another perk here at Bean Me Up."

CHAPTER 3

King City lights swarmed my vision as we drove in. Around us, the bustle of the city filled the streets, crowds pushing their way to their destination. Even this late in the evening, there were people everywhere. Joe rolled up the windows, but we could still hear the clamor come in from outside. As the wheels of the truck glided across the frozen pavement, my mind traveled back home. I surely hoped Mom was all right running the cafe on her own. I had asked fellow witch and my good friend Cilia to help but it still worried me to leave her unattended. That woman could burn the place down in seconds.

I shuddered, trying not to worry myself into a shaking mess in the front seat.

Joe brought the car to a stop in front of a boarded up convenience store and unbuckled his seat belt.

"The lounge is not too far from here," he announced. "Brian said there's no parking, so I hope you don't mind the walk."

As we made our way to the exclusive lounge Brian's friend reserved, I couldn't help but gape. The city was a far cry from Orchard Hollow. No one smiled or said hello and I had forgotten how easy it was to feel invisible here. It wasn't so long ago that I would have enjoyed the privacy, but lately, I had gotten used to prying eyes and gossiping mouths. Enough so to even miss them a little.

We turned down a dark alley and my nails dug into Joe's arm. "Is this right?"

"It's a speakeasy," Joe exclaimed. His hand stretched to point to a barely there neon light peeking out from around the corner. "Right there."

As we approached, I noticed an indistinguishable door in the wall that looked like any other alleyway back entrance. If not for the pointed arrow above our heads, I would have passed by it.

With a sly grin, Joe knocked on the door. There was a shuffle on the other side before a small compartment slid open at our eye level. Joe pointed his phone screen into the void and the compartment closed, the door bursting wide open a moment later. On the other side, a woman in a black and white suit stood with a warm smile on her face.

"Welcome to the Compendium," she announced. "If you follow me, your party has already arrived."

My jaw dragged on the floor as we marched down the narrow corridor.

Joe leaned in, his elbow nudging my side. "Pretty fun, no?"

"As long as we don't get murdered."

He laughed. "Only you would think that."

The hostess continued to lead us down a second corridor, which opened up to a large, rectangular space. Beautifully crafted tables filled the room, and the sounds of laughter and conversation drifted past us. Each table was taken; this place was popular. To our right, a large mahogany bar sat stocked with enough bottles to make any drink one could think of. The dark green Victorian wallpaper peered out from between mismatched frames, each one depicting people who died decades ago.

It felt like stepping back in time. The tables, made from rich, polished wood, held flickering candles in elegant holders that made light dance across the room. Above the bar, vintage chandeliers with crystal drops hung from the ceiling, adding to the room's already mysterious atmosphere. The bar itself was a master-piece, with its dark, glossy surface reflecting the colorful array of bottles behind it. Rows of glasses, from martini to whiskey, were neatly arranged, ready to be filled.

As I absorbed the details, I noticed the deliberate decor choices that brought the room to life. Plush, velvet cushions in deep reds and greens upholstered the vintage chairs at each table. Small potted plants and fresh flowers were strategically placed, bringing a touch of nature indoors and enhancing the overall charm of the place. I rolled my gaze over the place to take it all in.

It was magical.

"Right this way," the hostess said, pulling us forward.

We followed her to a round table near the rear of the lounge where two men were seated, deep in conversation. The first I recognized instantly from Joe's pictures. Brian was every bit the werewolf and exactly what I would imagine from a pack alpha. He had a close-cut beard that hid his wide chin and eyes so attentive they made you pause when he looked at you. His hair was longer, but he kept it tied back in a stylish man-bun, accentuating a jaw cut with a knife.

Across from him, a man dressed in clothes that I assumed cost more than the farmhouse sat with a

Cheshire grin spreading across his tanned face. His gray eyes looked us up and down and he leaned back into his chair, his lips curling. The only thing I thought of was how much Stella would love this guy.

"Joe! Piper! You guys made it," Brian exclaimed. He jumped up to shake our hands, and I didn't fail to notice that his friend didn't follow suit. "Traffic all right?"

"We missed the worst of it," Joe said.

He pulled out my chair, and I slid into it, gulping down the glass of water Brian poured to battle the awkwardness inside me. The sounds of mixed conversation and glasses clinking made my nerves hike and if I was honest, I couldn't wait to get to the hotel we booked and spend a quiet night away from home.

"This is Tyler Khan," Brian said, pointing to the snooty guy at the table. "Don't let the suit fool you. He's actually not so bad."

Brian reached over to pat Tyler on the shoulder and I saw the art collector break into a laugh for the first time since we sat down. His shoulders dropped and his entire demeanor changed before our eyes. Heat flushed my neck and cheeks. Gran taught me not to judge people based on their appearance, and here I was, doing just that. Tyler invited us all the way here and the least I could do was give him the benefit of the doubt.

I stretched my legs under the table and tried to relax. "It's nice to meet you," I said. "And I have a friend who would love that suit."

"Oh?" Tyler's brows hiked. "Does she live in the city?"

She does not live at all. I coughed into my hand. "Not quite."

Right at that moment, a server joined us, relieving me of further embarrassment. I let Joe and Brian order the drinks since I had no idea what some of the concoctions on the menu were, though the collector reassured me that they had the best gin in the city. Whatever that meant.

When the drinks arrived, I understood.

I picked up the sprig of rosemary garnishing my crystal glass. "It looks amazing."

"Told you," Tyler said with a wink. "Best gin."

"Are you excited about the exhibit?" I asked. "Brian mentioned it's highly anticipated."

At that, Tyler leaned across the table, beckoning for the three of us to inch closer. We obeyed, our heads nearly touching as he whispered, "This can't leave the table, but I have an ace up my sleeve."

"Oh, please!" Brian said. "You say that every show."

"No, truly, this time I mean it." Reaching for his tie, Tyler loosened the knot, his eyes sparkling. "I may have secured an exclusive piece. One that has been lost to the world for decades."

I was about to ask him more about it, but he kept on.

"As a matter of fact, why don't you three join me in the studio after the show?" he asked.

Brian slapped a palm on the table. "A private tour, huh?"

"Something like that."

After we all agreed to the plan, I finally took a sip of my drink, my taste buds dancing. If this is what Tyler meant about the best gin, I was here for it. In fact, I decided to corral Joe into stopping in a local shop to pick some up to take home before we left on Sunday. The night played on. All of us got lost in conversation and banter. Despite my earlier discomfort, I started to enjoy myself, the drinks playing a part in that, no doubt. Whatever the reason, I was glad we came out tonight.

This trip was exactly the break I needed.

CHAPTER 4

I f you were to ask me what I expected from a big, fancy art gallery opening in King City, this would not have been it. In fact, the spectacle Joe and I stood in the midst of was so far off the mark I couldn't have dreamed it.

"Better duck," Joe whispered.

I followed his advice, pushing my head down to let the ribbon dancer overhead have clearance to swing. The woman, dressed head to toe in red sequins, glided effortlessly through the air, her arms and legs flipping in the silky fabric that held her up. To our left, hands pushed out of a wall of leaves, handing out champagne for the guests. Next to it, a mime twirled cotton candy on an antique machine while a creepy clown made inappropriate balloon animals in front of him. The two seemed to be in some sort of stand-off and when I walked between them, I was pretty sure I heard one of them growl.

As I said, a spectacle, to say the least.

Yet, in the center of the over-the-top performances was also real beauty. It hung on the walls, stood in well-lit corners, and covered every inch of the art gallery. My jaw was unhinged for almost the entire evening as we took in piece after piece, admiring the art.

Each painting, sculpture, and installation had intricate details and vibrant hues that drew the eye. Some pieces displayed a sense of calm with their soothing palettes and gentle curves, while others were bold and dynamic, with large jagged forms and vivid contrasts.

My favorite was a deconstructed painting of a woman where every speck of paint was a tiny flower petal if you looked close enough. The artist had meticulously crafted each petal, layering them to create the illusion of a whole image from a distance, yet revealing an astonishing level of intricacy up close. Of course, there was also the main piece that took center stage at the opening. The special painting Tyler bragged about hung on its own wall with nothing around other than a single red rope partitioning it from the rest of the gallery. It was inlaid in an intricately carved gold frame that sparkled in the overhead spotlights. Inside, the most exquisite landscape I had ever seen painted drew me in. It was dark and moody, haunting in a way that made my body ache. Stunning, truly.

The gallery itself was an artwork, with its high ceilings and spacious layout allowing each piece to breathe. Soft lighting accentuated the colors of the works and invited everyone who passed to linger a tad bit longer.

In every corner, there was something new to discover. The gallery was full of surprises and for the most part, I enjoyed all of them. There was an energy to the night, a rapid increase of excitement that seemed to overtake everyone who entered. That, combined with the smell of patchouli wafting from one of the guests, made it overwhelming. I had to check on my skin several times simply to make sure my magic didn't come out to play in response to all of the raw energy surrounding me.

But it truly was something spectacular.

My eyes landed on a big, gaudy bronze sculpture of a tiger in a tutu in the center of the room. *Can't win them all.*

I hadn't realized we moved near the drink wall until an arm sliced across from me, the champagne flute nearly going right through my skull. Yelping, I jumped out of the way. The act drew the attention of several people who all watched me with a disgruntled look on their faces.

"At this rate, you may as well grab a balloon and start twisting."

I choked on my saliva. A wild cough broke free of me and my throat burned as I regained my breath. Head spinning again, I turned from Joe to confront a familiar face that I had no interest in seeing. Speaking out of the corner of my mouth, I said, "Stella! What are you doing here?"

"Hi, Stella," Joe added quickly. "Welcome to the party."

"A party indeed. This is lively," the ghost replied.

My teeth chomped down on my tongue. "Seriously, why are you here?"

"Why not?" Stella said with a scoff. "I used to go to art shows all the time back when I was alive. I missed the scene."

A juggler on a unicycle rolled past us, the wheel running over Stella's ghostly foot. She cursed under her breath, vanishing only to re-materialize in the same spot.

I laughed. "You missed that?"

"Perhaps not that, no."

The next hour flew by in a flash. We mingled with some of the other people attending while I tried to ignore Stella's unwanted commentary. A little while into the evening, Brian finally arrived and took the time to introduce us to a few of his friends. It appeared he and Tyler went way back since there were people here they had known since college. As Brian maneuvered us toward another group, a thought occurred to me.

I looked at Joe, pulling on his sleeve to get his attention away from a particularly captivating painting. "Hey, have you seen Tyler?"

"Um, yes. Hang on." He searched the crowd, pushing himself up on his toes to get over their heads. Eyes zeroing in on his target, Joe pointed to the far corner of the room where Tyler stood across from a man I hadn't met yet. The two appeared to be arguing and even from here I could see the red, angry splotches on the back of Tyler's neck. Joe frowned. "There he is."

"Looks like a heated exchange."

He nodded grimly. "The dark side of the art world," he said. "I bet they're talking about a sale."

The man raked his fingers through his silver beard and pushed his face close to Tyler's. He said something that made the art collector wince and I watched his fingers tighten around the piece of paper he held, his knuckles white as snow. Earlier, Brian said that his friend would be schmoozing potential clients all night and I wondered if this was a deal gone wrong. The art world was so far from my understanding that I had nothing to go by other than assumptions. In the distance, Tyler flattened out the piece of paper, smoothing it out carefully. He took out a pen and scribbled something on it, shaking the man's hand.

"Deal done," Joe said.

My lips formed a silent O. "How do you know?"

"That's the client list he's writing on," Joe exclaimed. "From what I recall in my days of attending these, Tyler wouldn't put anyone on it that didn't commit to a purchase." When he noticed my confused expression, he added, "Trust me, you're not missing much. It's all business from here on out."

Another couple joined us at the bar table we occupied and it was surprising to find out Joe knew them. I often forgot that he had an entire life prior to moving to Orchard Hollow, one that was very much involved in the city. I wondered if he ever missed the hustle and bustle of the place, not that we didn't get our share of excitement at home.

I cringed, remembering that some of that involved unlikely murders.

Gaze scanning the room, I tried to locate Tyler to thank him for having us, but he seemed to have disappeared again. Now that I saw the gallery, I completely understood his earlier demeanor. It took a specific persona to fit in with all these different types of people and to do it well. I had to hand it to Brian's friend—he pulled off something quite miraculous tonight.

I was enjoying myself and my normal idea of fun involved a cup of coffee, a book, and a room that only I occupied.

Polishing off another sip of champagne, I smiled when the bubbles went straight to my head. Beside me, Stella stood in silence—big shock to everyone—admiring a gargantuan stone sculpture of a man and a woman entwined in ropes. I leaned into Joe's shoulder and he slipped his arm around me, pulling me in close. Not even the ribbon dancer who continued to threaten to smash into me could ruin the evening.

It was absolutely perfect.

CHAPTER 5

Tyler Khan's studio was located a few blocks from the main gallery space in a part of the city that bordered on the residential. We walked down the tree-lined street in silence, reading the numbers on the two-story brownstones that filled the area. There were a few colorful mailboxes nailed to posts in front of the homes and it instantly reminded me of home. It was lovely to see that the city had not lost all its charm yet.

The barren trees were lit up with twinkling lights and there were planters with wreaths attached to them between each one. The streetlamps cast a yellow glow over the serene space, making me wish to stay here far longer. If it wasn't for the snow that started to fall and the fact that I forgot my mittens in the hotel, I'd have opted out of the studio tour and taken a long walk instead.

For now, this brisk jog down the adorable lane would have to do.

"Cute spot for a studio," I said, taking it all in.

Brian smiled. "There's a small warehouse down the block," he said. "It used to be a storage facility that Tyler's uncle owned. The place closed down years ago and Tyler bought it off him, turned it into an art studio to house all his collections between shows."

"Wow."

"It's not as impressive as it sounds. He lives there too," Brian said. "Most of the time."

Blowing hot air on my hand to keep it warm, Joe tucked both our palms into the pocket of his coat, saying, "I take it he travels a lot."

"Comes with the job," Brian said. "It's how he's able to secure special pieces like the one we saw tonight."

I thought back to the gilded frame, and the landscape portrayed in the painting it held. The haunting tone of the art came back to me in a wave of emotion, knocking my breath away all over again. Brian was right, that painting was quite special. No wonder Tyler was so excited about showing it off. I bet it had an impressive price tag attached to it, too.

As we walked, the homes became more sporadic, their placement further apart from one another. At some point, even the trees ended, and we followed the sidewalk to a darker, less populated part of the street. On the left, another building appeared, this one shaped like a large box made of brick and metal. There was no signage to indicate the destination, but judging by Brian's quickening steps, I assumed we had arrived.

Skipping up the single step, Joe raised his hand to ring the doorbell, but Brian waved him off.

"No need," the werewolf said. "Tyler never locks it when there's company coming."

We waited until Brian pushed the front door open and walked in to follow. It was surprisingly dark on this level of the building and it took me a moment to adjust my eyes to the low light. Brian and Joe had no trouble and marched through the place without so much as knocking into a wall. Since not all of us came equipped with vamp and werewolf sight, I had to stumble with my arms extended to avoid impaling myself accidentally.

"Put those flappers down," Stella said from behind me. "You look ridiculous."

I blinked, my eyes narrowing to take her in. "Should have known you'd show up."

"A private art tour?" Stella scoffed. "Of course I'd be here. Now, where is the good stuff?"

I padded lightly and carefully, following the direction Joe and Brian disappeared to. Up ahead, the space seemed to open further, and I saw glimpses of canvases stacked against the wall and a few flowing sheets over what had to be statues. As I inched closer, I noticed a large projector screen on one wall and a flickering light dancing across it. My head turned to follow the direction of the light, spotting a turned over projector lying lamely on the floor. Odd.

I glanced at my familiar and the look of concern that grew over her stoic features. "Strange, no?"

"Where's everyone?"

What an excellent point. I twirled on my heels, trying to find Joe and Brian, but the two seemed to have vanished. My ears perked as I tried to listen closer, my body stilling when I heard hushed voices coming from somewhere behind the projector screen. I exchanged twin looks of worry with Stella, then made my way toward the sound.

With two fingers, I pulled the screen to the side, shock raking through my body when I saw that the screen was actually covering a doorway. Slipping in behind it, I walked into the tight, cold room that lay ahead. My skin broke out in goosebumps even under the layers of clothes I wore. It was almost as cold in here as it was outside, a direct opposite to the room I just left.

"This must be where he keeps the more expensive pieces," Stella said.

When I quirked a brow at her, she added, "Temperature control. It's an art vault."

Nodding, I walked further into the art vault. Only a second passed when I was hit with a blinding light coming in from inside. I hissed like Harry Houdini when I blasted him with my magic, rearing away from the obnoxious beacon in front of me.

"Piper," I heard Joe call out. "Stay where you are. Don't come in here."

"You should definitely go in there," Stella rebutted.

Since by now Joe knew I'd do the exact opposite of what I was told, especially when it involved butting my nose into places, I followed my familiar's advice. With a few long strides, I sunk further into the vault, my heart dropping to the floor as I reached Joe. He stood in the center of a metal-enclosed area, his brow creased so deeply the wrinkles appeared painted on. Next to him, Brian wore an expression of horror, his gaze on the floor. I followed his eyes, a gasp breaking free of my chapped lips.

Lying at the men's feet was Tyler Khan. Half his body was trapped under the grotesque bronze sculpture from the gallery opening, the tiger in the tutu crushing the man entirely. His eyes were closed and I could tell from where I stood that he wasn't breathing. That he hadn't been for quite some time. There was a piece of paper clutched in his hand and I recognized it as the same list he carried with him at the opening. The sales list of potential clients.

A chill ran down my spine as the reality of the scene hit me. Tyler, the man who had been alive only hours ago, now lay lifeless and cold. I felt my knees weaken, threatening to buckle under the weight of the horrific scene before me. The air seemed to grow thicker, harder to breathe, as panic tightened its grip around my lungs. I shook out the wild energy of my magic that was clinging to my skin, blue electric sparks hitting an overturned chair in the corner. The magic singed the fabric and Joe had to stomp it out before I set the place on fire.

My heart raced in my chest, pounding so loudly it drowned out every other sound in the room. "W-what happened?" I stammered, my voice barely a whisper, trembling with fear and disbelief.

"We're not sure," Joe said. "He was already gone when we walked in. Brian called the police. They should be here soon."

"Brian, I'm so sorry," I whispered.

The werewolf barely heard me. His bloodshot eyes didn't leave his friend, phone still clutched in his trembling hands. "I wouldn't touch anything," he instructed. "The police will want to examine the crime scene."

"Crime scene? You think this was intentional?"

Brian didn't answer. I peeled my gaze away from him to look at Joe, who only pointed to a glass case a few feet away from the art collector's body. Atop the case lay an intricately carved gold frame that I recognized immediately. It was the same one that held the pièce de résistance Tyler boasted about at the opening. There was only one thing different about this particular frame.

The art inside it was gone.

CHAPTER 6

There were so many flashing lights on the street outside the studio that it almost looked like Christmas came early. I huddled in the front near the door, listening to the sound of boots shuffling and robotic voices from radios. Everywhere I looked I saw police officers. Apparently, Tyler's death was so remarkable that one team wasn't enough; they had to bring in the entire cavalry.

I couldn't help but gawk at how different the scene was from the times I'd ended up in very similar situations back home. Had we been in Orchard Hollow, I'd be getting a stern talking to from the town sheriff right now instead of being ignored in a corner.

Hovering next to me, Stella kept a watchful eye on

the officers who came in and out of the studio, their faces giving nothing away. Every once in a while, she broke her silence to make a snide remark, then returned to her post. I didn't have to guess at what she was doing; Stella was playing the same part as I was—gathering as much information as we could while we were here.

Somewhere further inside, Brian and Joe gave their account of what had happened. Since I arrived later than the two of them, my interaction with the lead detective didn't last as long and I was sent away to wait for Joe to finish so we could leave. Which was fine by me since it gave me a chance to gather my thoughts and figure out what in the coffee happened tonight.

I waited until the officers crowding my personal space left to take care of something inside the vault and turned to Stella. "Have you been able to make out anything important?"

"Don't start this, Piper," the ghost warned. "You're supposed to be taking a break. Playing makeshift detective is not a vacation. Besides, it's the holidays."

Methinks the lady doth protest too much.

I slanted my brows and waited.

"No, nothing about the death," Stella finally said. *There's my familiar.* "They seemed as surprised as we all were to find the art collector. Gruesome way to go."

I had to agree. Now that I had some time to get my

thoughts in order, all I could picture was the awful statue crushing Tyler. I didn't know if that was how he died, but if I had to guess, I'd wager it had a lot to do with it. Shivers tripped down my spine, my pulse racing. Surely there were easier ways to steal a piece of art. Or less horrible ones.

I shuddered.

Unless it was an accident. Perhaps whoever stole the painting came here thinking Tyler wouldn't be around. As far as I knew, he hadn't told anyone about the tour he offered us, so it stood to reason that the killer would believe the studio to be empty. If they came here with the intent of stealing the work, there was a good chance Tyler had caught them off guard. People did dumb things when they were surprised. Some even killed.

"Do you think it was an accident?" I asked Stella.

The ghost poked her head down the studio toward the vault. "Quite possibly so," she replied. "I doubt anyone would plan to kill with a tutu tiger."

"That's my thought too. More likely they came here to steal the art, not expecting Tyler. Maybe there was a struggle, and the killer used whatever they had in arm's reach to get away."

"The art collector certainly talked a lot about that painting," Stella added. "Anyone could have over-heard him."

I scratched my neck until I could feel my skin heat up. "And everyone at the opening knew how much it was worth. It was the star of the show," I said. "But how would they know to look here?"

"They would if they knew Tyler well."

Right as the wheels started turning in my head, they ground to a halt. My eyes grew watching Brian stalk out of the vault, his hands in fists at his side. The werewolf growled deep in his chest as he walked toward me, stopping between me and the front door.

I opened my mouth, then closed it again. For once, I didn't know what to say.

"Joe knows some of the officers from back in the day," Brian said. "He'll be out soon after he says his goodbyes."

I should have known that Joe's past life as a defense lawyer here in King City would mean he was acquainted with the police. Something told me that he wasn't hanging back for good old small talk. Joe was probably doing what me and Stella were and trying to gauge what may have gotten Tyler killed while he had the chance. The detective bug must have rubbed off on him while dating me. Call me odd, but I kind of liked it.

"I should get home," Brian said.

Tearing myself from my thoughts, I looked at the werewolf, my heart breaking. Brian looked completely destroyed. Not only that, but he was going home to an empty house to wallow in sadness alone. I couldn't let him do that.

Placing a hand on his shoulder, I said, "Why don't you wait and Joe and I can join you?"

"No, no," he answered. "It's your last night in the city. This was probably not what you expected to end the trip on, but you should still make it count. I'll be fine, I promise."

"I'm really sorry for your loss."

The werewolf smiled, but it didn't reach his eyes. "Thank you. I didn't see Tyler as much as I'd have liked. He was a good guy, one of the few left from our old group. I still can't believe he's gone."

I gave his shoulder a light squeeze, though it did little to bring the warmth back to Brian's face. There was nothing I could do to make that happen. As someone who had lost a loved one fairly recently, and had seen her fair share of death, I knew only time would heal Brian's wounds. This was one case when a werewolf's speed healing could not help.

Sometimes being a paranormal made no difference at all.

Footsteps sounded behind us and glanced over my shoulder to see Joe approach. Though he didn't know Tyler, I could see the night took a toll on him as well. How could it not? It was the first time I met the art collector, and I was shaken to the core. I could only imagine what Joe and his good friend were going through.

About to offer my sympathies, I stopped when Brian interrupted.

"I was just telling Piper that you should try to make the best of the night," he said. "I can recommend some good spots for a late dinner."

Joe's lips down-turned. "That won't be necessary, I'm afraid," he said. "The police want us to stick around for a while longer."

"In the studio?" I asked.

There was a long silence, followed by Joe's frustrated exhale. "In the city," he breathed out. "We can't leave town until they clear us."

CHAPTER 7

I woke up in a cold sweat with the sheets wrinkled and tied around my legs like cotton ropes. It was still dark outside the hotel window, the morning sun yet to break on the horizon. Despite the early hour, I could hear people clamoring on the street four stories down; everyone starting their day and was oblivious to the tragedy that occurred last night.

I turned over and paused when my hand touched a cold, empty pillowcase. Shooting up in bed, I searched the room for any sign of Joe but didn't find him anywhere. My eyes closed tightly. It took me a moment to gather the energy to get up and throw a hotel robe over my nightgown. It was the fluffiest thing my skin had ever touched, and I melted into its cozy cocoon.

With slow, careful steps, I pulled the sliding door of the bedroom and stepped out. Outside the sleeping area, the suite was much brighter thanks to the wall-to-wall windows on one side of the room. There was a narrow couch against another wall with a modern, abstract framed print hanging over it, a giant mounted television across the way, and a glass coffee table between that I was certain had seen its fair share of stubbed toes.

I found Joe standing in front of the windows, looking down at the city below with a solemn expression casting a dark gloom over his features.

"Couldn't sleep?" I asked.

Joe bristled before turning around. His eyes were red and his hair was in a state of messy reserved for mornings after too much drinking. Tyler's death had a bigger effect on my boyfriend than I realized. I thought Joe only met the art collector recently but was starting to doubt that right now.

"I was on the phone half the night with Brian. Stepped out, so I didn't wake you," he explained. "You seemed like you needed the rest.

Ah. There it is.

I forced a meek smile that barely tugged at my lips.

"I'm sure you could have used it too," I said. "How is Brian holding up?"

"He's getting through it. As well as can be imagined, I suppose."

"They were really close, huh?"

Joe shrugged, moving past me toward the coffeemaker in the room. Without asking if I needed one—because who were we kidding?—he pressed a button and the machine whirred to life. Joe placed a paper cup under the nozzle and waited until it finished pouring before handing it to me. The coffee tasted of plastic and sadness, but I gulped it down like a starved beast, regardless.

"Brian isn't like other werewolves," Joe said. "He feels more. Almost as though he imprints on every person he meets. It's what makes him such a good PI; he really digs into things. He does the same with his friends. Losing Tyler so abruptly shook him. Especially since it's so close to the holidays."

I sucked in a slow, ragged breath. "Did Tyler have a big family?"

"You know, I'm not sure. I told Brian we'll meet him for lunch today so we can ask then." His eyes met mine. "I hope you don't mind."

"Of course not," I replied. "Not as though we're going anywhere any time soon."

Joe gave my shoulder a squeeze and excused

himself to get ready. I suggested he take a power nap before we head out for the day, but he refused. Somehow, I understood why. This was one way Joe and I were very similar; both of us couldn't sit in one place when our minds were racing.

As I watched him sneak off into the bathroom, I made a second terrible hotel coffee and settled in on the couch. My attention flicked to the television, then to my phone resting on the coffee table. Without a second thought, I picked it up and pulled up a search bar. As expected, the news of Tyler's passing had already hit the online papers. There were no reports beyond what we already knew—that the art dealer was dead and a priceless painting was missing.

Well, not priceless. Quite the opposite, actually.

I scrolled through the posts, finding nothing that piqued my interest. As far as the media was concerned, Tyler's death was a tragic event surrounded by a fog of mystery. In other words, no one knew what happened. Which was odd considering how many people were at the art opening. Surely, someone must have witnessed something out of the ordinary that could help the police track down the killer and thief.

I threw the phone down with a resolved groan. *Nope. Not getting in the middle this time.*

"Not my circus, not my monkeys."

"Unfortunately, you're still dressed like a clown."

I jumped, my hand pressed to my chest at the sound of Stella's voice. Continuing to clutch my chest until I regained my breath, I deadpanned on the snooty woman. "A little warning next time, please."

"Here's a warning," Stella rebutted. "You should answer that."

"Answer wh—"

My words fell away, the phone I tossed away ringing off the hook. I arched a brow at my familiar, who only pretended to inspect her nails in return. Rolling my eyes, I checked the screen and fumbled with the buttons to pick up the call. "Mom? Hey. Did you get my message?"

As I listened to my mother speak, my forehead increasingly wrinkled. By the end, I looked like a poorly folded fitted sheet tossed at the back of a linen closet. My lips parted, teeth grinding as I ended the call. Leaning against a window, Stella stood limned in the light of the rising sun, her face beckoning for answers.

I put the phone down and said, "The cafe is in trouble. Mom is in over her head." I shook my head. "Harry ate an entire box of cupcakes, then threw up on one of the front tables. Right in front of the window during a rush."

"Teaches you right for leaving your mother in

charge," Stella said, as though I didn't guess my mistake. "If you have any hope of keeping your business, you better hope the police solve this case fast so you can get back home."

Nodding, I turned away from her to look out the window. Golden rays hit my eyes. I swiped at them when they started to water. As my vision blurred, I could think of only one thing: how absolutely right Stella was. My cafe was my baby, and I had to make sure it survived the wrath of Sylvie Addison.

There was only one thing to do. I had to move the investigation along if I had any chance of keeping my livelihood. The police in King City may have been good at their jobs, but there was one thing they didn't have working for them. A half witch-half ancient deity spawn determined to find out the truth.

CHAPTER 8

We met Brian in a busy part of the city at a cafe not unlike Bean Me Up. When we approached, the first thing I saw were the quirky mugs stacked to resemble an Alice in Wonderland tea party, and I was hooked. Peering into the snow-frosted windows, I spotted a large Christmas tree in the corner with flashing lights and precious ornaments strewn throughout. There were even wrapped presents under it; for the employees, I wagered. The cafe had the same type of charm I worked hard to keep up in my own establishment. The charm I desperately hoped Mom wasn't destroying in my absence.

After Joe finished getting ready, I filled him in on

the phone call. I also mentioned that I thought we could use our special abilities to help guide the police in the right direction to speed up the process of the investigation. It took some convincing, but after a while, reluctantly; he got on board. A quick reminder from Stella that my abilities were basically electrocution, seeing dead people, and butting my nose where it didn't belong set me straight. Since Tyler's ghost was nowhere to be found, we would have to do this the old-fashioned way.

Joe opened the door and led us to a table near the front window of the cafe where Brian was waiting.

Luckily, we had a private investigator on our side.

I pulled out a chair and sat down next to Brian. "This place is great," I said. "And it smells amazing."

"They have the best sandwiches in all the city. And an all day breakfast selection." He handed each of us a menu. "The salmon benny is my favorite."

After putting in our order, we chatted for a bit about topics I found hard to follow. I believe the weather was mentioned several times as was everyone's plans for the new year. I tried to keep calm, but deep down, I was crawling out of my skin. For a moment, I started to wonder if Joe filled Brian in on our plan like he said he did. At this rate, we'd be getting the bill before we had a chance to discuss what happened to Tyler.

I was about to give up on the idea entirely when Brian reached into the leather satchel hanging on the back of his chair and took out a manilla folder. He laid it on the table, pushing our empty plates aside—the benny was, in fact, heavenly—and opened the front flap. Inside, there were printouts of at a dozen black and white photos. Each one was fuzzy and low in quality, as though it was taken on a security camera.

"This is everything from the security footage the night of the gallery that shows Tyler in frame," Brian said.

Well, there you have it.

I picked up half the pile while Joe took a stab at the rest. "Thanks for doing this," I told the werewolf. "I know you're putting your neck on the line here."

"No need to thank me. Tyler was my friend. If I can help catch whoever did this, I'm happy to help." He pointed to one of the photos in my pile with his index finger. "This was at the start of the night. You can see Tyler more in these, but he stopped showing up on cameras after about nine."

"He disappeared?" Joe asked.

Brian took the photos from him and flipped through them until he found what he was looking for. "Not exactly. He was gone for about an hour, but came back later. Right here."

I studied the photo, comparing it to the ones in

front of me. Tyler's hair was ruffled, like he had run his fingers through it a few too many times. He was also wearing a different blazer. I distinctly remember the bright red jacket he wore when we first saw him because Stella made sure I knew the name of the designer who made it. Yet in the photos Brian spread before us, Tyler's blazer was dark and covered in what seemed to be black sequins.

My lips puckered. "He changed clothes."

"You noticed that too, huh?" Brian asked. "I saw the same thing. Only thing I could think of was he spilled his drink and had a spare at the gallery."

"Or someone spilled it on him," Joe suggested.

My ears burned at the implication. "You think he got into a confrontation with someone that went south?"

As Joe nodded, a memory from the night flashed before me. I leafed through the pictures frantically, searching for the part of the night I recalled. It took a bit of time, but after a lot of squinting and several paper cuts, I found it. Turning it around to face Joe and Brian, I said, "We saw Tyler arguing with this man when we came in."

Leaning over the table, Brian brought the photo close to his face, then pulled away. He reached into the folder again, this time producing a piece of paper with names typed up in small font on it. There were too many for me to make out, but Brian seemed to know what he was after.

"That's the gallery owner," he said. "Andrew Wells. I didn't realize they didn't get along."

"It did look confrontational," Joe admitted. "I thought it was a sale going down, but I could have been wrong."

Sliding the list toward us, the werewolf PI tapped on the paper twice. "This is the guest list from the night. Take a look and if there's anyone that you recognize, let me know."

I doubted that we would know the people from the opening enough to point them out, but checked, anyway. Joe found the couple we ended up spending the night talking to and another woman that was very interested in a photograph collection from a local artist. Other than that, we had no clue who any of those people were. While the men continued to discuss the list, something came to me that didn't sink in before.

Someone on that list was the killer.

I pulled the paper closer, resting it next to the photograph of the gallery owner. And there was a very good chance that we already knew who it was.

CHAPTER 9

"Would you like a bag? Miss?"

I shook my head out, the thoughts rushing through my brain fogging up reality. My attention refocused on the man behind the counter holding out a stack of books. Head tilting, I tried to recall the question, but nothing came to mind.

"A bag?" the man repeated. "For the books."

Heat clawed its way up my neck. I grabbed the books and crammed them into my purse. "Oh, no, thank you."

"Hope you found everything you need," the man said. His silver hair hung low past his shoulders, a streak of blue running down the right side. He twirled his nose ring, watching me. "There's a signing event this weekend that you should check out."

I smiled, tucking the books I picked up for Joe deeper into my bag.

"That sounds lovely. But I don't think we're staying that long."

Or I hope we're not.

I thanked the man for his time and slipped out of the store, keeping my eye out for Joe across the street. We had decided to spend the day touring King City in a pathetic attempt to avoid the thing we both wanted to do most—talk to Andrew Wells. After lunch with Brian, I was convinced that the gallery owner was up to no good. The argument we witnessed at the opening didn't appear to be a normal occurrence. Tyler was visibly upset and no matter what Joe originally thought, it was quite obvious now that it wasn't a sale.

Something else was going on and it quite possibly had to do with the art collector's death.

A flash of red caught my eye as Joe crossed the street toward me. He held up a giant cup with a coffee bean logo on the front and steam billing off the top. I melted at the idea of a coffee.

Joe handed me the cup with a nod. "Find anything?"

"Perhaps," I said, wiggling my brows. "It's a

surprise." Biting my lower lip, I added, "Listen, I've been thinking..."

Joe surprised me with a sly, devious grin.

"If we catch a taxi now, we can be at the gallery in twenty minutes."

About to ask him how he knew what I was thinking, I stopped when Joe lifted a hand to hail a car. There was no need for ride shares in King City; it was one of the few places that still mainly functioned on good old-fashioned taxi drivers. As Joe's arm waved, three yellow cars sped our way, and I had to jump away from the curb as one skidded to a stop in front of us. There were a few angry honks from the other drivers, but they sped away when Joe opened the back door to let me in.

The taxi driver, a woman in her mid-forties with hair the color of fire, looked over her shoulder as we piled in. "Where to, folks?"

Joe and I exchanged knowing glances.

"Baker Street Gallery," I said. "As fast as you can get us there, please."

If there was anyone in the history of driving that understood the assignment more, it was impossible to tell. The woman wove through the densely packed streets of the city with the ease and speed of a fighter jet pilot. We took to narrow passages that I thought were alleyways and cut through lanes I didn't realize were equipped to handle car traffic. In the windows, the outside world blended together as she picked up speed, getting us from the city center to the gallery in fifteen minutes flat.

My head spun as we climbed out; legs regaining their balance on solid ground.

Before us, the gallery loomed like a dark, monstrous thing ready to swallow us whole. All right, fine. It wasn't all that melodramatic, but it certainly felt that way to me. I specifically told myself that I would stay out of murder investigations and yet here we were. In my defense, being Hades's daughter kind of meant that death followed me around, often in the form of dead bodies or the spirits of those recently passed.

Unfortunately, this time the only spirit around was that of my familiar, who happened to be floating in front of the gallery's front doors. I watched as the ghost's tennis skirt, the outfit she did it in, floated in the wind, and shivered. Feeling instantly foolish, I brushed the empathy away. Stella could not get any colder, really.

Nudging my head to the door, I said, "Stella is here."

"Hi, Stella," Joe said. He pulled the door open and stepped aside. "After you, ladies."

"What a gem," my familiar said as she floated past me to get inside first.

I groaned. When we walked into the gallery, the first thing I noticed were the bare walls surrounding us. Gone was the art that was here less than twenty-four hours ago and the only thing left to remind us of the evening were the tags on the walls where the names of the pieces hung before. I knew that items that were sold were moved to the studio at the end of the night, but I was under the impression that the rest of the pieces would remain.

My gaze traveled over the blocks of white paint, searching for an explanation.

"If you're here for the show, I'm afraid it's closed indefinitely," a voice called out from the rear of the gallery.

Our necks stretched to see over the side of a random display wall in the center of the room. Beyond it, a man in his fifties approached, his gray coveralls covered in fresh white paint. He held a brush in one hand and a painter's mask in the other. Despite his casual appearance, there was no mistaking it. This was Andrew Wells, the owner of the gallery we stood in.

Joe waited until the man was close to ask, "That's a shame. We thought it was on all week."

"It was meant to be," Andrew replied. "But there

were some unfortunate circumstances, and it had to close down."

"Do you mean Tyler Khan's death?" I asked.

The gallery owner stiffened. His neck muscles bulged and his knuckles grew white, matching his ashen skin. I had clearly caught the man off guard, exactly as I wanted. People who were flustered tended to talk too much, in my experience.

Casting a quick glance at Stella, who was floating around the gallery looking for clues, I kept on. "It's all right," I said. "Tyler was a friend of a friend. We were hoping to see the show one more time without so many people, but I suppose we missed our chance."

"Ah, I see. I'm sorry to be the bearer of bad news," Andrew said.

"Why did you cut it short?" Joe asked. "If you don't mind me snooping."

The gallery owner flashed his pearly set of teeth. It was jarring. Almost like seeing a wolf pull down his sheep's mask. "If I can be frank," Andrew started. What I learned from past interactions was that when people started with that statement, it often meant they were going to say something awfully insulting. I waited for Andrew to follow the same trajectory. I was not disappointed when he said, "This show was nothing but a money pit. Upsetting about Tyler, of course, but I'm relieved to have walls to fill again."

"I thought Tyler secured several remarkable pieces," I said. "Especially that one painting. What was it called?"

"The Walk at Dawn," the gallery owner replied. "That was the big problem. Tyler added that painting after we forged a contract for the show. If I had known he was going to present something so valuable, I would have negotiated a better price. It was tricky, what he did. Unfair."

I pushed the toe of my boot against Joe's. "Did you try asking him for a new contract? I'm sure Tyler would have been open to it."

"Ha!" Andrew hollered. "He certainly wasn't. Told me a deal was a deal and if I wanted more money, I'd have to talk to his lawyer. The nerve of the man." He rubbed the back of his neck until it turned red. "Look, I know he's gone, and that's awful, but I'm not sorry I took the show down. To be spoken to that way in my own gallery on opening night... he crossed a line."

So that was what the argument was about. Andrew tried to get more money out of Tyler and the art collector flat out refused. I wanted to think the best of Brian's friend, but at this moment, he wasn't looking so great. As much as I didn't appreciate the way the gallery owner was speaking of the dead, I sympathized with him. What Tyler did was a dirty play, and I'd have reacted much the same way had it been my business on the line.

I looked at the barren space we stood in.

Perhaps not as hastily, though.

"Anyway, sorry you came out all this way for nothing," Andrew said. He raised the brush he held in the air and waved it around. "I should probably get back to cleaning the place up. The next show is starting the day after tomorrow. You two should stop by."

"Thank you. We'll think about it," Joe said.

We left the man to his painting and stepped out in the winter cold. I waited for Stella to join us, but the ghost was nowhere to be found. She likely got bored and vanished to do whatever it was she did when she wasn't driving me insane. As we put distance between us and the gallery, I couldn't help but recall how Andrew spoke about Tyler. It was beginning to appear that the art collector was not the man he was pretending to be.

My belly turned.

What else was Tyler Khan hiding before he died?

"What are you plotting now?" Joe asked, his arm sliding under mine. "You have that look on your face."

I crooked a brow, slowing my step to peer up at him. "I have an idea, but you're not going to like it."

Joe sighed.

"Here we go again."

CHAPTER 10

J oe absolutely hated my idea.

It took me forever and a day to get him on board and even then I wasn't so sure he wouldn't back out at the last minute. Thirty minutes of pacing outside the gallery followed by a taxi ride, where he mumbled about how we were going to step in it this time the entire way. When the car stopped a block away from Tyler Khan's studio, I was convinced he would make it turn around to take us back to the hotel.

As always, Joe surprised me.

"Keep your phone on you," he instructed. "If I text, find a place to hide and stay there until I come get you. Do not try to sneak out on your own."

I traipsed behind him onto the quiet street. "Got it, captain."

"I'm serious, Piper. I'll keep the cops busy so you can poke around the place, but this isn't Orchard Hollow. If you get caught, there's no Romero here to bail you out," he warned. "I may know some of these people from back in the day, but I'm not a lawyer anymore. You'd be in deep trouble if they catch you in an active crime scene."

I nodded and kept my head down as we hurried toward the studio. There were several cruiser cars parked outside and yellow tape sectioned off the building from the remainder of the street. I spotted a news van idling by, but no cameras and no reporters hounding the police while they worked.

When we got closer, another face I recognized caught my attention. "Is that Brian?"

"I asked him to meet us here," Joe explained. "He can help distract the cops while you do your thing."

Seeing us approach, the werewolf waved and motioned toward the rear of the building—my way in.

I waited on bated breath as the two men approached the front entrance of the studio and walked inside. Casting a quick glance around, I made sure I was alone before following the way Brian instructed down the side of the building. The rear of the studio was industrial and barren. Gray brick rose high in the sky, obscuring the sun from view. A few pigeons gathered on the roof, watching me with beady eyes. There was a scratching sound near the single dumpster with its lid wide open.

I stopped dead in my tracks.

My breath hitched and my heart hammered away at a steady, fast clip. I sucked in a sharp breath and waited. And waited. And waited. The scratching stopped, light footsteps replacing it. They hurried toward me at an increasing speed. My pulse matched their beat.

Suddenly, a masked face appeared from behind the dumpster. A furry, curious face.

I let out a whimper, which turned into a nervous laugh. It was only a raccoon.

"You remind me of my friend," I told the creature.

It looked at me sideways, then scurried away again. When I glanced at my hands, they were glowing with electric magic and I had to shake them to get the energy to subside. This was already not the greatest start, but I had to keep going. I needed to see inside Tyler's studio, and this was my only chance.

Before me, the back door, clad entirely in metal, stood tall and intrusive. I tested the handle and relief flooded through me when I found it unlocked.

Thank you, Brian.

Slow as molasses, I opened the door and stepped

inside. My ears perked, listening to the sounds of the studio. In the distance, I heard a rumbling laugh and stilled. It was only Joe keeping the officers busy, no doubt. The plan was going well so far.

I skirted a corner and checked for the police before making a beeline for the stairs leading to the second floor. Brian mentioned that Tyler lived here and since I didn't see a bedroom when we first came by, I assumed the living quarters were sectioned off upstairs. My feet padded softly on the metal steps, each one igniting my nerves further. By the time I reached the top landing, I was a wreck.

"About time you got here."

My hand clutched my chest. I whisper-yelped at the jarring sound of my familiar's voice. Stella waited for me to regain my composure before saying, "Seriously, hurry up, Piper. The coast is clear, but it won't be for long."

I wrestled my hand away from the railing I clung to.

"Why are you sneaking up on me?" I scolded. "You almost gave me a heart attack."

"I figured this was your next stop."

I stepped further down the narrow hallway we stood in. "So you decided to scare the coffee beans out of me?"

"I decided to check the place out so you didn't waste time doing it yourself."

If I wasn't still trying to catch my breath, I would have hugged the frustrating woman. That, and if I were able to hug a ghost. Semantics. Instead of wasting more time chatting, I pointed down the hallway toward the three doors lining it. "Did you get anything?"

"Follow me," Stella said.

Moving at the speed of light, I ran after the ghost until we reached the furthest door on our right. Training my ears, I waited a few seconds and when I didn't hear anyone around, I opened the door and stepped in. The room we ended up in was bare bones save for a desk, a chair, and laptop riser without a laptop in sight.

"Tyler's office," I guessed. My gaze rolled through the space. "The cops must have his computer. Shoot."

Stella ignored me, floating down the side of the desk to point to the bottom drawer. "Look in there."

I did as she bid. The drawer pulled out with a creak, my stomach dropping into my boots. I was being way too loud. Calculating my next few moves carefully, I pulled out the stack of papers tucked inside and laid it out on the desk, checking each one. At first, it seemed pointless. But then my eyes caught on a list I knew I'd seen before. I gasped, yanking it out of the pile and spreading it out before me.

I turned to Stella. "The buyer list," I said. "From opening night."

"See anything strange?"

I followed her gaze to the slot reserved for the stolen painting, a knot forming in my throat. There was a name recorded, but it was scratched out, a second name written directly beside it in quick, rough scribble. The word "outbid" was printed beside it.

"What does that mean?"

Stella fixed me with a deadly glare. "Read the name."

"Marina Wallace," I read out loud. "That doesn't sound familiar. Do you think it's important?"

"That depends. Do you think the gallery owner's girlfriend outbidding someone for the main piece of the evening is important?"

My jaw fell to the floor. I scraped it up, tucking my tongue back in as the shock wore off. "Marina is dating Andrew?"

"Sure is. She came by shortly after you two left the gallery. I recognized her name when I was snooping." She blew on her manicured nails. "Did I do good or what?"

"Stella! You are brilliant!"

She scoffed. "It's about time you understand that."

Her pale eyes darted to the hallway outside. "Better make yourself scarce."

Shoving the papers back into the drawer, I shut it tightly and bolted out of the room and down the stairs. The voices I heard before were gone, replaced by the heavy steps of officers walking inside the building. I retraced my steps, moving like a cat burglar with agility I didn't realize I had. When I burst through the rear door, my palms were slick with sweat and my entire body vibrated with anxiety.

I half ran, half walked toward the front of the building, taking the corner a little too fast. My shoulder collided with a hard object, my body spinning around from the impact. The wind blew at my face and a musky scent filled my nostrils. I focused my spotty vision to watch the person I walked into, hurry away.

"Sorry about that!" I yelled after them.

They held up a hand, not bothering to turn around. "No problem at all. Watch your step. It's icy out here."

As I put distance between myself and the studio, walking toward the meetup point Joe set for us, I couldn't help but smile. We had a proper lead. It may have been icy outside, but things were heating up in my head. We were on the verge of breaking this thing wide open. I knew it.

CHAPTER 11

Surely most people should have a private investigator for a friend. Bonus points if said investigator was also a paranormal with a nose for sniffing people out.

It took Brian all of ten minutes to track down Marina Wallace. He followed her to a posh neighborhood on the north side of the city, overlooking the park. As we sat on a wrought-iron bench beside a well-cared for swan pond, I kept my eyes squarely on the four story townhome across the street. The natural stone building was limned by the bright sun behind it, standing amidst city traffic like a beacon. There were several windows on each floor punctuated by Juliette balconies and overhanging flower planters that were filled with tiny poplar trees. Delicate lights hung from under each planter, illuminating the detail in the iron design. Below the window, double doors stood front and center, another full planter on either side.

The sound of conversation and rising laughter echoed behind me. I turned, watching the passersby strolling the massive park I sat in. One couple carried an old-fashioned picnic basket, their eyes locked on each other in the way only new love allows. Walking after them, another couple worked to contain their three children who ran amok on the grassy hills, hiding and poking their heads out intermittently. Further back, a group of teenagers chatted loudly as they walked arm in arm down the winding path between the trees.

I smiled, my body settling into the cold metal of the bench.

"It's lovely here."

Next to me, Stella sighed loudly, crossing her long, slender legs. "This park was mine and Arthur's favorite place to visit in the city."

"Did you visit often?"

A darkness passed over Stella's face.

"Not as much as I'd have liked. More so than before—" she paused to retie her ponytail "—I died."

I opened my mouth to give her some encouragement, but before I could speak, the front door of the townhome flew open and a stunning woman stepped outside. She wore a long white wool coat, yet even under its weight I could see she was all curves and beauty. Her pale hair was tucked under a fur-lined hat that matched her coat and she sported a designer bag that hung off her arm effortlessly.

"That's Marina," I told the ghost. "We're up."

"Best get it over with before the vampire has a heart attack," she said, reminding me that Joe was waiting a few blocks away in a cafe. Between Stella and I, we managed to convince him to stay behind so we didn't ambush Marina. That didn't mean he liked the idea, though.

The ghost vanished, reappearing next to Marina in front of the townhome. Pushing off the bench, I left the city park and scurried toward the crossing, hopping along until I was close to Marina. The woman reached into her logo-encrusted purse to search for something. I took my chance.

Running up to her as fast as my trembling, nervous legs would take me, I all but threw myself on the unsuspecting woman. My hair flew behind me, red ringlets catching the wind and slapping me in the face when I skidded to a stop three feet from the door. A few pieces glued themselves to my lips thanks to a new lip gloss I tried after Stella's never-ending badgering that I put some makeup on that morning.

I spit them out moments before Marina turned around to face me.

"Um, hello?" she said, confused.

I feigned the warmest smile I could manage to battle the chill running up and down my bones. "Hi! Marina Wallace?"

"Sure..."

My smile widened to the point of verging on creepy. "My name is Piper Addison," I said. "I spoke with your boyfriend earlier. About Tyler Khan."

Marina's features froze.

"You talked to Andrew?" she asked. "When? And why?"

I side-glanced at Stella. the ghost shot me a curt nod and squared her shoulders. Her hips shimmied as she floated closer to the front door. "Keep her busy while I look around inside."

Somehow, I doubted she would find anything of value, but it was a good plan. Since we had nothing to give to the police yet, it was plausible that there would be evidence in Marina's townhome they could use. Perhaps even the stolen painting itself. But why bid so high on a piece if you had no intention of paying for it?

A memory of Andrew's anger toward getting a

bum deal flashed before me. Unless they worked on this together. If they got Marina to buy the piece, then stole it, they could collect insurance money to make back the price of the sale. I didn't know much about the art world, but I was certain a piece that expensive was insured. Were Marina and Andrew committing insurance fraud? And did Tyler catch on and pay the price?

"Hello?"

Marina's voice jarred me. I blinked fast, pushing the wayward thoughts away. "Sorry about that. I spaced out a little."

"Sure. So... Andrew?"

"Right, of course," I stammered. "I visited the gallery earlier. The show is taken down. Did you know?"

Marina nodded. "I did. Why does it matter?"

"No reason," I said. "The main reason for the show had already been sold, anyway. I was too late, I suppose."

The woman's eyebrows shot up into her forehead. One of her eyes twitched as she inspected me, looking at me clearly for the first time since I approached.

"You were interested in The Walk at Dawn?"

"My boyfriend and I entertained the idea," I lied. "But the final bid on it was way out of our budget. Whoever got it must have really wanted it."

Marina paled before me.

I leaned in, feigning concern. "Are you all right?"

"I-I'm not sure," she stuttered. The woman bit her bottom lip until I thought she'd chew it off. "Can I tell you something in confidence?" She waited until I nodded to say, "You dodged a bullet on it. The painting is gone."

I opened my mouth wide in mock shock. "Gone? Gone how?"

"Stole," Marina said. "And before you wonder, it isn't hearsay. I was the one who bid on it. Luckily, I hadn't sent a transfer to Tyler yet until he could get it properly secured. I'm sure you could imagine the paperwork that goes along with such a hefty purchase."

"Of course," I said. Though I couldn't imagine buying anything that extravagant. "I'm sorry to hear that. You must be devastated."

She shrugged. "Honestly, I'm relieved. I wasn't even supposed to shop that night. Andrew tipped me off ahead of time that a new piece was being added last minute," she explained. "He said it was supposed to be the find of the century. I'm a bit of a collector, you see, so I had to get my hands on the painting. But I won't lie. Spending that much on a new artist seemed fool-ish, even for me."

"I didn't realize the painting was done by someone

who wasn't famous. For that price, I mean." I stood back, a question swirling on the tip of my tongue. "Why would someone want to steal it if the artist wasn't even well known?"

Closing the distance between us, Marina leaned in, her lips close to my ear. To anyone passing by, we must have looked like two women gossiping. It was definitely how it appeared to Stella who chose that exact moment to pop up next to me.

Oblivious to the ghost's presence, Marina cleared her throat, whispering, "Don't tell anyone, but my money is on the daughter."

"Whose daughter?"

She pulled back, her brows furrowed. "The artist's. Stanislav Carr," she said. "From what Andrew told me, the painting was worthless until he died suddenly last fall. His daughter, Kierra, believed she was owed the piece since it was her father who painted it."

"Seems fair," I said.

Marina shook her head. "Not really. Tyler purchased it directly from Stanislav before he died, so she had no rights to it. If anyone was going to snatch the painting, it would be her."

My eyes moved past the woman's shoulder to Stella. The ghost gave me a thumbs up, agreeing that Marina was definitely onto something here. This was the first I heard of any daughter, but the timing was much too coincidental. That is, if everything Marina said was true.

I raised a questioning eyebrow at Stella, who frowned in return. She did not find anything of value inside the townhome. Not that Marina would store a stolen, priceless piece of art in the open, but my familiar could be very nosy when she needed to be. If there was anything to find, she'd dig it up.

The thought reminded me of Harry Houdini, which made me immediately remember the cafe. Time was running out.

We needed to find Kierra Carr and put an end to all this nonsense. And fast.

I looked at Marina, saying, "Your secret is safe with me. Looks like you're right about us dodging a bullet."

"We girls have to look out for one another," she said, though she didn't know me, nor had she done anything to truly look out for me. She wiggled her fingers in my face. "Anyhow, I must get going."

I wiggled mine in return. When Marina was down the street and out of sight, I turned the corner and walked to the cafe where Joe waited. Behind me, Stella floated silently, taking in the views as we passed. As much as I would have loved to sightsee with her, I kept my gaze low and my steps quick. My mind reeled with possibilities, theories that all jumbled together into a big web.

Kierra Carr was the answer. I didn't know how yet, but that was the whole point.

I was going to prove it.

CHAPTER 12

"What do you mean she doesn't exist?" Joe pressed the phone closer to his ear and listened intently. His lips formed a thin, tight line. "Hang on, let me put you on speaker so Piper can hear."

He pressed a button and put the phone on the small dresser in the hotel suite. After a clearing of a throat, Brian's voice filled the room. I leaned in to hear him better, an unnecessary choice, since the werewolf was so loud he was almost shouting.

"I mean, she doesn't have a record anywhere," he explained. "No credit cards, no social media, not even an email account associated with the name Kierra Carr."

I bristled. "That's odd. Marina was adamant about the name. Maybe she got it wrong."

"Or she changed her last name?" Joe suggested.

On the other end of the phone, the line went silent. A moment later, the sound of typing broke the quiet lull as Brian worked his magic. Not his actual magic, only his impressive skills as an investigator. As he licked away, I shoved the last of the chocolate chip cookies we brought back from the cafe into my mouth. The taste overwhelmed me as the chocolate melted and coated my tongue in sweet deliciousness. I chased it down with an oat milk latte and sighed. I was really missing the Eggnog Cappuccinos from Bean Me Up. If it wasn't for this hold up, I'd have been enjoying one right about now and helping Mom with the dinner menu instead of chasing down women who clearly didn't want to be found with a werewolf and a vampire.

Though I had to admit, out of all the terrible things that have happened since we got into the city, spending time with Joe has been lovely. And getting to know Brian better was a good bonus as well. He was a good friend of Joe's and considering how much he had to put up with the people in my life, it was nice to return the favor.

A sharp inhale drew my attention back to the phone. "I think I have something," Brian said. The keys clanged rapidly again. "You were right, Joe. She goes by Kierra Stone now, switched it ten years ago. There's more under this title, but not much to go on."

"Is there a social media profile?" I asked.

"Hang on."

We waited patiently, our feet tapping wildly in unison. An excruciating length of time later—a few seconds, really—Brian finally spoke. "Got it. Sending you the link right now, Joe."

The phone vibrated and slid across the shiny marble dresser top. Both Joe and I reached for it, our foreheads bumping hard. I yelped. Joe hissed. The matching bumps on our heads swelled.

Rubbing the sore spot, I stretched my hand slowly, waiting for Joe to back up before snatching his phone. I clicked on the link the werewolf sent and waited for the site to pull up in the search tab. Brian was right, there wasn't much to go on here. Either Kierra was incredibly private or she didn't exist before last year, when her social media started popping online.

I scrolled through the pictures, my eyes carefully dissecting every detail of the young woman. She had a meek demeanor, I could tell even without having met her. Every photo of Kierra showed her with her slim shoulders hunched and her eyes looking anywhere but at the camera. Her dark hair hung down the sides of her face. On anyone else, the hairstyle would have helped frame their features, but Kierra looked like she was using it to hide from the world.

I flicked past a few more photographs and stopped on one showing her standing next to an older man. Despite the age gap, the resemblance between them was uncanny.

"This must be Stanislav Carr," I said, proceeding to read out the caption below the post. "My father and his masterpieces." I turned the phone around so Joe could glimpse it better. "Looks like they're in a studio of some sort."

"Likely the artist's work space."

I nodded, inspecting the photo in closer detail. "Is it me, or do they look as though they only met for the first time here? They're not even hugging."

"Some people aren't huggers."

"No, she's correct," Brian said.

His voice ringing loud on the speakerphone jarred me. I had almost forgotten he was on the line. When he spoke again, I realized why he was so quiet before. While we were ogling Kierra's profile, he was researching. "Stanislav left his family to travel the world and paint when Kierra was still in diapers. The two didn't reconnect until recently."

"That would explain why she changed her name. I wouldn't want anything to do with a man who left me either," Joe said.

My thoughts darted to my mother, and I shook them away. *This is not the same,* I reminded myself. Mom left to keep me safe, not for any other reason. Still, I couldn't lie and pretend it didn't sting to this day despite knowing the truth now. Though having her back had been helping mend the bitterness that swelled in my chest from time to time.

Reaching for my own phone, I found Kierra's profile again and opened up a new message. An invisible string pulled my lips up as I typed. Next to me, Joe quirked a bushy brow, looking down the length of his nose. "What are you doing?"

"Just sending a friendly message," I said. "As someone who admired Stanislav Carr's art, I'm offering my condolences on his death."

"Why would you do that?"

My smile stretched further, my bottom lip disappearing. "Because it would be odd if I asked her to meet me out of the blue. She might not want to meet a stranger," I explained. "But she might give up a sliver of her time for a longtime fan. Especially someone who just offered to buy some pieces from her at a very exorbitant price."

CHAPTER 13

Kierra Carr never bothered to reply to me. Not only that, but she didn't even check her messages. Almost a full day had passed and with the sun setting, I doubted there was much we could do now. Our only true lead was leaving us hanging. To make matters worse, Joe got a call from a friend on the King City police force that pretty much confirmed what I already suspected— they hit the same dead end as we did.

My head pounded, a headache careening from temple to temple. There was no way I'd be home in time to save my cafe, let alone back for the holidays, at this rate.

The sound of rising conversation drifted around

me as I aimlessly folded the cocktail napkin in front of me. Next to it, a half-drunk martini stood waiting, the glass dewy and sparkling. I twisted around on the barstool and searched the hotel bar for Joe. When I spotted him walking toward me, I called the bartender and ordered a second drink.

I had the distinct feeling that even though Joe wouldn't drink, I may need the liquid encouragement tonight.

My eyes flitted to the tall black marble fireplace in the corner of the vast room. The fire inside crackled and hissed, a reddish hue cast on the tastefully arranged garland strewn over the mantle. Above it, a modern centerpiece of a winter village all clad in white stood upon fake snow-covered hills. The windows of the tiny buildings twinkled with lights and a vise locked over my chest.

I really didn't wish to miss Christmas in Orchard Hollow.

Joe pressed a hand to the small of my back as he slid onto the adjacent barstool. "bad news," he said solemnly.

I frowned. *Of course. More bad news.*

"I just got off the phone with Sevi from the force and it seems they don't have anything to move the investigation into Tyler's death forward."

"Did you tell them about Kierra?"

He nodded. "They already had her on their list. Nothing to show for it though."

"They can't find her either, huh?"

"Not exactly," Joe said. "They went by her home, but she refused to talk. Sevi said their hands are tied until they have enough evidence to bring her in. Which might be awhile."

The lines forming around my lips and eyes deepened. "We're stuck here indefinitely, aren't we?"

"I'm afraid so," Joe said. "I'm sorry. I know you were keen on holidays back home."

More keen on keeping my business open. My lungs refused to expand fully as I attempted to take a full breath. This was an absolute nightmare. My hands tingled, and I had to shove them under my butt to keep my magic from making an unfortunate appearance. The anger inside me bubbled to the surface with little I could do to contain it. I couldn't believe I was once again stuck in the middle of a murder investigation. Coffees blast you, Hades. Dear old dad made me a magnet for death and there was nothing I could do about it.

Whether I liked it or not, this was going to be the rest of my life.

I could already feel my mood souring entirely, ruining a perfectly decent night in the city. It wasn't until Joe spoke again that the grip the rage inside had on me, loosened.

"I did get Kierra's address, though," he said. When my face brightened a few shades, he winced. "Perhaps I should have led with that."

I chuckled. "No kidding. How did you find it?"

Joe stretched his fingers, his knuckles cracking. A roguish grin tugged at his lips.

"You're not going to tell me, are you?"

His grin spread and his Adam's apple bobbed when he asked, "Do you want to rehash the details or do you want to talk to the artist's long-lost daughter?"

I sucked back the last of my drink and slammed the glass on the bar. Grabbing my coat from the hook under the counter, I tugged it on, buttoning it up as quickly as possible. My eyes met Joe's. You don't have to tell me twice.

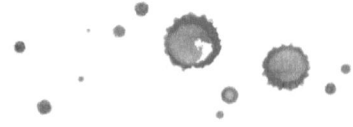

We walked hand in hand down the street the taxi dropped us off on. To anyone else, we looked like a couple enjoying a nice evening stroll. In reality, we were on our way to ambush a possible killer and I was using Joe for balance because I almost broke my neck twice slipping on snow.

Romance was in the air.

Or was that garbage? The street had a distinct aroma that made my stomach turn.

"I believe that's it," Joe said. He pointed to a five story building up ahead. When we walked up and checked the names on the buzzer, he quickly noted Kierra's last name. "That's her."

I reached for the button, but he stopped me, my arm hanging in midair. Joe nodded to the side of the building, where a column of fire escape ladders stretched all the way to the roof. The metal structure sat close to the building, holding onto the dark brick for dear life. Joe pulled at my sleeve and I followed him until we stood beneath a rusty pull-down ladder.

I looked up the length of it, shuddering. "You can't be serious."

"Sevi said she hung up on them each time they tried to buzz up. If you wish to talk to her, we need to get in there and knock on her door. Don't give her a chance to shut us down."

I blew out a long, exhausted breath. Pointed to the ladder. "How do you propose we get this thing down? It's pretty high."

With a curt nod, Joe stepped away from me and jumped up in the air. His arms stretched up and for a second, he appeared to be flying. I knew he wasn't, but his vampire strength made him get so much momentum a human would rarely mistake the two. It was quite impressive. That was until Joe's fingers wrapped over the rod at the base of the stairs and nothing happened. He hung from the metal contraption, a look of concern coating his features.

Frustrated, Joe gave the staircase a tug, but it didn't budge.

"Well, shoot," he hissed out.

A laugh fell out of my mouth, which earned me a disappointed glare. I shook out my hands, saying, "Hold on tight." Then I blasted the top of the stairs with my magic.

The electrical current that poured out of me zapped at the metal, shaking it violently in the night. At the base, Joe's fingers strained as he held on. A moment later, the staircase came loose and was flying down at an increasing speed. Joe jumped out of the way seconds before the bottom hit the ground with a clang.

We both cringed.

"Let's hope no one heard that," I said.

"Better make it quick."

We climbed the rackety metal stairs two steps at a time. My fingers froze against the railing and I had to pause periodically to blow some heat back into them. I followed behind Joe, trying not to look down as the ground disappeared beneath us. The further up we went, the more the wind picked up, and I had to watch my step to avoid slipping on the ice formed on parts of the metal.

Joe came to an abrupt stop above me. My head knocked into his butt, pushing him upward. I grimaced. "What's going on?"

He held up a hand. I took it, climbing up three steps to be at his level. Joe's gaze was locked on the two tall windows stationed on this level. I followed his eyes, my stomach dropping into my boots.

"That's Kierra's place," he whispered. "I'm certain of it."

The pit in my belly grew until I tasted bile. It rose up my throat, coating it and making me gag. My feet faltered, knees knocking together as disappointment set in.

The apartment we peered into was entirely emptied out. Stanislav Carr's daughter was in the wind.

CHAPTER 14

This was definitely the end of my life.

I stood in the center of the bridge, the bustle of tourists and people local to the city shuffling by me. Not far from me, Joe took photos with his phone to send to my mother because she would flay him if he returned without documentation of our trip. Those were literally the words she used when I called her earlier to check in.

While Mom was busy worrying over Joe's phone gallery, I was nearly in tears thinking about her recounts of the cafe. They had to shut down early almost every day this week because the local bakery supplying us with food was shut down for the holidays and no one knew to find a backup. Not only that, but

Mom was not exactly a trained barista and without Rory to help out, all she could make for people was drip coffee and tea. She suggested she start adding liquor to both. I vetoed that idea faster than I could expel a breath.

The last thing I needed was for the sheriff to close me down for illegal alcohol sales.

Although, Mom was doing a stellar job at getting the cafe close to shutting down all on her own.

I couldn't blame her entirely, which was likely the part that stung the most. I never should have left. Who decides to go on random trips a week before Christmas? I rolled my eyes. This Twiddle Dee, that's who.

My eyes traveled past the thick metal railing encasing the bridge and to the water below. The city was surrounded by it. So much so that had it not been for the small sliver of land attaching it, King City would be King Island instead. In the summers, people came from all over to experience the busy city shoreline. Back during my short stint of living here before settling in Orchard Hollow with Gran, the water was my favorite part; this spot was, in fact, my most visited attraction. And yet it did nothing to make me smile.

All I could think about was how we let Kierra slip through our fingers.

Well, that's not quite true. I was mostly wondering if we should look at short-term rentals since the police were intent on ruining the holidays for us. I frowned. Surely they would find the killer soon and we could finally be free to leave.

I turned around, leaning on the railing, the wind rustling my hair. A second whoosh of cold air blasted my face, and I turned in time to see Stella Rutherford materialize next to me. The ghost folded her arms across her chest as she checked out the scenery.

"Cute place," she said. "Great view."

It took me a second to realize she wasn't talking about the bridge or the water. Stella's eyes narrowed as she brushed them over, Joe approaching us. His wool coat flapped behind him as he walked, the muscles of his chest taut with each step. I shoved a fist through my familiar's shoulder.

The ghost yelped.

"Stop drooling."

She shrugged, but averted her gaze slightly. Now she had one eye on Joe and one on a random stranger passing by. It was unnerving.

As Joe came to stand before me, the ghost said only one thing. "Tell him to pick that up."

I did a double take.

"The phone, Piper."

"What are you—"

I stopped talking when Joe's phone rang in his hands. His brows met in the middle as he looked at the screen, creeping closer together when I said, "Stella says you should get that."

"How did she—"

I held up a hand to stop him. "Don't ask," I said. "I don't have the slightest clue."

Fumbling with the buttons, Joe picked up the call, putting it on speaker. It took a moment for the phone to connect and when it did, there was a loud, ear-piercing screech on the other line. I hissed between clenched teeth. Joe growled.

Stella... did not react one bit.

"Hello?" Joe asked.

Another loud screech was followed by buttons being pressed randomly. Then a familiar voice said, "Joe, hey. Brian here."

"Brian? What's that racket?"

The werewolf huffed out a slow breath. "I'm trying to wrap up at the office and my alarm system chose this moment to crap out on me." Another screech had Brian cursing under his breath. "Look, I'm going to send you something right now you need to see. I dug more into your artist's daughter and an interesting photo came up. You'll have it shortly."

We exchanged glances and huddled closer together to watch the phone. As Brian promised, a text from him popped on the screen within seconds. Not waiting, Joe clicked on it and enlarged it on the screen.

My jaw fell open.

The image was of two people sitting on a wooden bench. Behind them, a building with a bell tower in its core rose high into the sky. I brought my face closer to the young man and woman and the graduation garb they wore. Each of them held a rolled up diploma, and they were so happy they bordered on delirious.

I swallowed the lump that formed in the base of my throat. "Is that Kierra and Tyler?" I asked.

"Sure is," Brian replied. "They went to high school together, if you can believe it. It's odd, he never mentioned it. But maybe it's not important."

I begged to differ. This was vital. I didn't know how yet, but it couldn't be a coincidence that Tyler came upon Kierra's father's art piece by chance. And for her to start talking to her dad after years of being estranged was even more bizarre. Could Tyler and Kierra have been planning something together? Perhaps Kierra double crossed the art collector and things spun out of control.

Leaning in even further, I tried to pinpoint what bothered me about the photo. It wasn't right, but like everything else concerning this case, I had no clue how.

That didn't matter, though. We needed to talk to Kierra Carr, now more than ever. If only we knew where to find her.

CHAPTER 15

"She won't reply," Joe said. He watched me type out yet another message to the woman that did not wish to be found. "She ran for a reason."

I sighed. "We don't know what her reason is yet."

"Murder looks pretty good," Stella suggested.

Features darkening, I shot the ghost a deadpan glare, finished the message, then said, "What happened to innocent until proven guilty?"

"Innocent people don't run."

Mom did.

I put the thought away, packing it away with the remainder of my doubts about my mother. Who also showed up out of the blue after years of being gone.

Much like Kierra. My thoughts swam. Mom returned because she needed help with a wicked coven set on destroying the world, the same coven she had been hiding me from. What if Kierra had a similar reason for speaking to her father again? And what if that reason is why she was gone now?

Things didn't quite add up. We were missing a vital piece of information and I hated that I couldn't figure it out.

I tapped a finger on the top of the nightstand, aimlessly. "Do you have the pictures from the gallery opening?"

Joe threw his legs over the side of the bed we lounged upon. He walked out of the bedroom, wrestling with our suitcases in the front of the hotel suite. As I waited, I tried to make sense of all the ideas swirling in my head, but I couldn't get a grasp on one distinct pattern. All I knew was that there was something we missed. Something vital.

"What are you thinking about?" Stella asked.

I spun to face my familiar right as Joe plopped the folder of security footage photographs in front of me. "I'm not certain," I admitted. "Call it a hunch."

"I think I speak for Stella and I when I say that we trust your hunches," Joe said.

Standing before the dark window, the ghost nodded approvingly. I opened the folder and flipped page by page, my attention splitting between every detail. I noted the people, what they wore, where the art was and the time when each person entered the gallery. I even counted how many drinks people had when I had the chance to spot a glass in their hands.

Then I made two piles.

I worked quickly, separating the photos left and right. From either side of me, Joe and Stella watched in silence as my brain worked to create a timeline of the evening. Perhaps if we knew where every guest was, we could trace Tyler's steps better, even when he wasn't in the pictures.

Leaning back, I looked at the piles. "Wait," I whispered.

Giving it one more go, I added a third pile to the mix, reshuffling the glossy papers until I was satisfied.

"There," I said.

Joe grimaced. "I'm sorry, I don't think I follow."

"These are the ones Tyler was in," I said and pointed to the first stack. "These are everyone else. And these—" I drew the last stack closer "—are all of Kierra. Now let's see what we find."

We worked in tandem. I pulled out a photo and Joe scribbled the time noted on the bottom right corner from the camera on a piece of paper. Picture by picture, we began to reconstruct the evening with as much detail as the evidence before we could provide. I inspected each image so closely that my eyes hurt by the time we got to the last one.

I rolled my shoulders, my spine uncurling. "What do we have?"

"It appears that Kierra arrived shortly after the doors opened," Joe said. He tapped a thick finger on a grainy image depicting both Tyler and the artist's daughter. "I think this is the first time they talk."

I glanced at the black-and-white photograph.. "They look friendly."

"They should," Stella added. "They'd known each other for years."

We retraced the woman's movements through the night. Each time, referencing them back to Tyler to see how they matched up. In every picture that showed the two interacting, it was nothing but smiles. In a few, they were even hugging. Nothing about this pointed to a feud, not until... I pulled out a photo and flattened it out on the bed cover. "What happened here?" I asked.

In the photograph, Kierra was shooting daggers at Tyler with her eyes. The image was taken later in the evening, after Tyler came back from being gone a while. Her posture had changed—straight and stiff— and there was a new expression covering her prior cheerful features. It looked almost like fear.

"Check this one out," Joe said.

He handed me another photograph, one I missed

before, since it only captured Kierra's back near the front door. "Is this when she left?"

Joe nodded.

"Huh," Stella mused. "Right after the strange interaction with Tyler. Odd."

I agreed. There was a deep-rooted strangeness to the evening. Did Tyler and Kierra argue? Was it over the painting? Or perhaps money? It was impossible to discern, since we only had pieces of information and the woman who could help fill them in was nowhere to be found.

"You should go to the high school," Stella said.

I did a double-take. "The high school Tyler and Kierra went to? Is it even in the city?" I glanced at Joe, realizing he only heard half of that. "Stella is suggesting we talk to the school."

"It's a good idea," Joe said. "Let me see if Brian can get us an address."

He stood up again and walked out to get his phone. While he was gone, I spread the photos out on the bed, my head tilting left and right as I worked to memorize each one. My memory wasn't what it used to be, but I did a good job at taking a mental screenshot of what I could.

A throat cleared in the doorway. I looked at Joe, his face pale.

"What happened?"

"I just got a call from the lead detective on Tyler's case," he said. "They arrested someone for the murder."

My eyes bulged so hard I thought they might pop. "Who?" Stella and I yelled in unison.

"Andrew Wells. There's a hearing in two weeks and they need us around to testify."

The world got a little quieter. Outside the window, snow fell as a winter storm gripped the city in its icy fingers. A shiver tripped down my spine. My mouth slacked, my head not comprehending what was happening. The police had the wrong guy. There was no way Andrew was the killer, I was certain of it. To make matters worse, the hearing was well past Christmas. My cafe and my sanity would not last that long.

I swallowed the hard lump in my throat, but it only bobbed up and down, choking me.

This was an epic disaster.

CHAPTER 16

King's Crown Collegiate was a quaint school situated a short drive from the city, and in the surrounding suburbs. Nestled between a residential park and a shopping mall, the high school was the epitome of a building that forgot its purpose. Not quite big city and not quite small town. There was a tennis court on the far right of the school that hid behind a tall, metal fence with ivy running up it in swirling tendrils. Next to it, a big industrial concrete space sat empty save for a few bicycles left beside a bench. Past it and up the narrow driveway lined with short trees, was the school itself.

Joe pushed open the wide double doors for us to

enter. They groaned behind me, squeaking with age. When we called earlier this morning, we were advised that school was shut down for the holidays, but we were more than welcome to stop by and speak to one of the staff members still here. We kept our reason for the visit vague to avoid scaring anyone off. I wasn't sure what the protocol was for divulging student information from decades ago, and we couldn't afford to risk having the door slammed in our faces.

As we entered, the darkness of the place made me buckle back. Not only were there very few windows in this part of the building; it appeared someone had forgotten to turn on the lights.

"Christmas break," Joe said.

I squinted to make out the poorly lit hallway ahead. "I think the office is this way."

Pointing to the only room in the hallway to emanate light, we made our way past rows of lockers at a brisk pace. As we walked, the smell of paper and cleaning solvent permeated my senses, instant memories of my own high school days flashing before me. It had been ages since I stepped foot in one and being here was bringing it all back. Strange how a place could do that. Recall.

I rubbed my thumb over the photograph of Tyler and Kiera that I brought with me. Hopefully, someone here would remember as well.

We neared the open doorway and stepped inside. My senses immediately went into overdrive. Bright lights blinded me, making my vision spot at the edges. The blaring holiday music blasting through invisible speakers had the hairs on my arms standing on edge. I looked at Joe, who was cringing so hard his eyes had formed thin slits.

"What is happening here?" I asked as another voice shouted, "Hello? Come around back!"

We followed the woman's instructions. Skirting around the wide reception counter of the office, we traipsed by tall stacks of labeled boxes, past stacks of papers piled so high they formed a wall, and all the way to another door in the rear of the room. Inside, a woman in a purple sweatsuit carried several more boxes to add to the mix, the top one barely balancing. She dumped the boxes to the floor with a thud, wiped her wet brow, and turned to face us.

"Coffee be damned," I whispered through my teeth as the woman's face came into view. Her thick-rimmed glasses obscured some of her features, but there was no mistaking her. "Kierra Carr?"

The woman, Stanislav Carr's daughter, cocked her head to the side to inspect us. She inched closer, stopping when she noticed the photograph hanging limply in my hands. Her eyes traveled up my body, landing on my rounded eyes. "I haven't gone by that name in ages," she said. The tremble in her voice was hard to miss. "You're her, correct? The woman that's been trying to get a hold of me about Tyler?"

I nodded.

"We're sorry to barge in," Joe added. "Though in our defense, we didn't realize you'd be here."

"I help out at the school from time to time," she explained. "Have been since after college. The extra money is nice and I like being here. Brings back good memories."

My gaze darted to the picture. "Of you and Tyler?"

Kierra nodded.

"Is there a reason you won't speak to the police?" Joe asked. "I get that we're strangers, but they're trying to find out what happened to your friend. Unless..."

"Let me stop you there," Kierra said. Her arms crossed over her chest and her glasses rode down on her pointed nose. She huffed out a short, stubby breath. "I know what you're going to insinuate, and no, I didn't kill Tyler. I would never."

I shoved the photo in my coat pocket. "Because you were friends?"

"Because he was basically family. He was the reason that my dad and I started talking again," she said. "If he didn't sign him as a client, I never would have even known where he was. Dad and I, we didn't have the best relationship growing up. Tyler knew all about it and did his best to help."

"He connected you two?"

"Sure did," Kierra said. "And I was grateful for it. It meant a lot to see my dad before he passed, to make things better somehow. It didn't fix the years of anger I had for him, but at least I could say we tried in the end." She paused. Looked around. "So, no. I didn't kill my best friend. And no, I won't answer any of your questions. I'm not talking to the press."

Shuffling my foot, I nudged Joe's boot with the toe of mine, clearing my throat. Kierra's eyes shifted left and right like that of a wild animal caught. Her voice pitched higher when she spoke about Tyler and you could tell by the color draining from her face that things were off. Kierra Carr was afraid. That was why she ran. That was why she ignored all my messages. That was why she refused to help the police.

Which only led me to one conclusion.

I buried my gaze on her. "You know who killed Tyler, don't you?"

"You need to leave," she said.

Next to me, Joe started to speak, but I cut him off before he could make things worse. If there was anything I understood in this life, it was what it meant to lose someone you loved. I also deeply got the effect that fear could have on a person; the paralyzing aspect of it. Kierra didn't need to be convinced to talk. All she needed was someone who told her it would all be all right..

I smiled warmly, taking a step back to give her some space. "We're not journalists," I said quietly, my hands up in surrender. "We knew Tyler. He was a good friend to our good friend. All we want is to find out who did this to him and make sure they don't do it to anyone else. If you help point us in the right direction, we promise to keep your name out of it until it is safe."

She didn't seem convinced.

"Please, Kierra," I begged. "Help us."

The woman stared at me for a few moments. Her pupils dilated, and she narrowed her eyes, trying to make a decision. She may not have been convinced by my speech, but at least she didn't look like she was about to run anymore. After another minute of excruciating silence, she sighed and said, "Come with me."

Nodding to Joe, I followed Kierra out of the office and down the hallway. My heart beat wildly in my chest as we walked past the lockers to a wall I paid little attention to upon entering. There was a large wooden display case sitting against it full of trophies and framed photos of past students in their glory days. I pressed my nose to the glass, not understanding why she brought us here.

Her shoulders hunched, Kierra reached for a switch on the wall and the lights above the display case came on. She pointed to one particular photo of a newspaper clipping. It was yellowed with age but held up pretty well, all things considering. In it, two boys in soccer uniforms held up a large bronze trophy, both with wide smiles on their faces.

I gasped.

"That's Tyler," Kierra said. "And his twin brother, Ethan. They won a few trophies for our school that year. But that was before Ethan went off the rails."

My throat was suddenly dry and full. I tried to speak, yet no words came out. The shock of the discovery rendered me mute. Luckily, Joe didn't have the same problem because he said, "My friend would have known if Tyler had a twin brother."

"Tyler cut Ethan off years ago. Right after he stole from their mom," Kierra explained. "The boys didn't come from money. Single mom, dad not in the picture. It was what brought us together as friends at first. Tyler always wanted to make something of himself so he could pay their mom back for everything she'd done for them."

"And Ethan?"

Kierra scoffed. "Ethan only cared about Ethan. We were still in high school when he started stealing. First from the neighbors, then from strangers. When he emptied out their mom's savings to buy a car, Tyler lost it. Made her kick Ethan out of the house and told him not to come back. They haven't spoken since." She stopped to look down the hallway. "Not until a few weeks ago."

I exchanged a quick glance with Joe.

A door slammed somewhere behind us and Kierra jumped, her hand clutching her chest. My stomach muscles tightened. "What did Ethan want?"

"Money. What else?" She grimaced. "He saw the articles online about my dad's art piece and wanted a cut. Tyler sent him packing."

"But he didn't leave, did he?" Joe asked.

Biting her bottom lip, Kierra checked the hallway again. It was as empty as before, though she continued to monitor it, worry creasing her brow. "When I saw him show up at the gallery, I got the hell out of there. That guy was always trouble. I wanted nothing to do with him."

My body froze. The long period of time Tyler was unaccounted for. The change of clothes. It all made sense now.

I bit the inside of my cheek, then let it go. "That was Ethan we saw in the security footage at the end of the night."

The three of us stopped moving and turned to look at the framed article in the display case. We didn't have to speak for the question on everyone's mind to be apparent. It hung in the air, oily and vile, a poison on the tip of our tongues.

If Ethan Khan was the one who returned to the gallery that evening, what happened to Tyler?

CHAPTER 17

Before we left the high school, I convinced Kierra to do us one final favor and after some push back, she reluctantly obliged. It took a lot of promise on both mine and Joe's part to keep our end of the bargain and not speak a word of her involvement until she felt safe to do so. In other words, until Tyler's killer was behind bars.

Ethan Khan was going down.

I shook my hair out and the thought with it. There was no need to get ahead of myself yet. We still didn't have any proof that Ethan killed his brother and stole the painting; a problem I was hoping to solve now that we had Kierra's help.

Standing in the shadowy entrance of Tyler's

studio, I watched Joe fill the police in on our plan. This was one time it proved useful to have the cops to help, and I was relieved that we didn't have to do this alone. I was even more relieved that no one arrested us for interfering with the investigation behind the scenes.

As it turned out, when Joe said he had friends on the force, he really meant it.

He patted one of the officers on the shoulder and walked toward me, closing the door after him. When it was only us in the dimly lit studio space, I finally dragged in a solid breath.

"All set," Joe said. "They'll wait for my signal to come in and will stay out of sight."

I looked at the vintage watch I inherited from Gran. "Ethan should be here any minute."

"If he takes the bait."

My chest tightened. There was every chance that Ethan would ignore Kierra's message. Though I highly doubted it. When I asked her to text him after years of not speaking, she was confused. It wasn't until I explained that I wanted her to pretend to need his help that she understood. The plan was for Kierra to confide in Ethan that the art piece Tyler had was a decoy, a fake to keep the real art safe until the final transfer of ownership post buy. She went on to tell him that now that the police deemed it stolen, she didn't want the attention on her. That she needed money, and she needed it fast.

I asked her to lay it on thick, to play to his ego. And Kierra stepped up to the task. She even had me convinced that she truly believed Ethan was the only person she could trust to sell the art under the radar. That, combined with the promise of splitting the sale, made me certain he would be here.

My eyes locked on the small hand ticking around the watch face. "We should go further in so he doesn't see us immediately."

We were about to scurry into the shadows of the studio when the door creaked to open. My lungs expanded. I held in a breath, sweat pooling at the base of my back. Behind me, Stella said, "Don't worry," seconds before Kierra's face peered through the opening of the door.

"What are you doing here?" I asked. "It's not safe."

The woman stood up a little straighter, her hair tied into a tight bun. "You're going to need me. If you're right and Ethan is the killer, he won't be easy to deal with. I can help talk him down if he gets agitated."

I started to argue, but the sound of heavy footfalls outside made me clamp my mouth shut. We all looked at each other before diving into the long hallway leading away from the front door. Backing up further, we made sure we were hidden enough that Ethan wouldn't see us immediately. Then we waited.

Joe took the front while Kierra and I huddled next to him. I poked my head out around his shoulders and narrowed my eyes, keeping them locked on the doorway. A few feet ahead, Stella did the same. I knew she only stayed behind for solidarity since she could quite literally walk through the wall and see who was coming. My heart warmed at her sudden urge to be part of a team.

Before us, the door handle twisted and light streamed in from outside, briefly filling the studio. I inhaled sharply, praying to the coffee gods that Ethan didn't see us and run. Luckily, he kept his eyes down on the ground as he locked the door with a definitive click.

He slowly made his way into the depths of the studio, and I couldn't help but gawk. It was uncanny how much he resembled Tyler. The photograph we saw at the high school made the two boys appear similar, but with slight differences. Tyler's hair had a wave to it while Ethan's was pin-straight and fell past his ears in limp strands. Their noses also were a bit off. Where Tyler's was straight and stoic, Ethan's had a bump at the base that made it look more round. But now, here, I couldn't tell them apart if I tried. If someone asked me, I'd have said that standing before me was none other than—

"Tyler?" Kierra shrieked from behind Joe's wide back. "W-what? H-how?" She stopped talking, her face ashen. "I don't understand."

"That makes two of us," Stella agreed.

Slowly, the man entering the studio inched toward us. His gaze followed Kierra, who had crept out from around Joe and stood in the hallway a few feet from him. The smell of patchouli hit me smack dab in the face. I coughed, my eyes growing wide as moons. I recognized that smell from the gallery and then from the other day when I snuck into the studio. The person I knocked shoulders with on the way out was Tyler. I'd know that smell anywhere now that I knew who it belonged to. He must have returned to the studio to make sure he covered all his tracks. I was so foolish not to have realized it sooner. If Harry Houdini was here, I bet he'd sniff out the traitorous killer in no time.

Tyler's eyes drifted past her to Joe and me huddling close together. "Why are they here? I said to come alone."

"Are you kidding me?" Kierra shrieked. "That's what you're worried about? Tyler, people think you're dead. What are you doing here? And why do you have Ethan's phone?"

She broke away to clear some distance between them. Kierra's arms stretched out as she neared Tyler, ready to hug him. Next to me, Joe must have had the same realization as I did because he jumped to attention. Using his vampire speed, he caught up to Kierra in a flash, grabbing her arm and yanking her backward—away from Tyler. He twisted, pushing her behind him once more, his eyes feral.

"What are you doing?" she asked, starting for her friend again.

This time it was me who pushed her back. "Stay away from him," I warned. "He killed his brother. Don't think he'd hesitate to kill you, too."

"That's ridiculous. Tyler, tell them..."

Her words fell off, lips trembling as she wrapped her fingers around my arm in a grip tight enough to hurt. I turned around in slow motion. The sound of a gun's safety being pulled reverberated in my ears and I had to stop myself from screaming as I stared down the barrel of the revolver Tyler pointed at us. My hands shot up involuntarily. Kierra did the same.

The only one who didn't flinch was Joe. His chest puffed out as he said, "Put that thing down. You don't need any more blood on your hands."

"What do you know about it?" Tyler hissed out. I couldn't help but note how different he sounded now than from that first night we met him. Although perhaps my hunch to not trust the guy had been right all along. Tyler's nostrils flare. The gun stayed up. "I don't know why you two got involved, but nobody's walking out of here."

"What did you do?" Kierra breathed out.

"What I had to." Tyler raked the long fingers of his free hand through his wavy hair. "I was broke, Kierra. About to go bankrupt. I didn't have a choice."

The woman holding me in a vice grip loosened her hold. "So you killed Ethan? Why? Help me understand. Please."

"He wasn't supposed to die," Tyler said. "After Ethan contacted me asking for money, it got me thinking. That painting, your dad's greatest masterpiece, was worth millions. And what? Some random girlfriend of a stuffy art gallery owner was going to get it? For what? To hang in her living room and collect dust? I couldn't go through with it. So when Ethan reached out, I asked him for help."

"To do what?" Kierra asked.

Tyler's jaw tightened. The cut defining it sharp enough to slice through glass. "The plan was to switch places halfway through the evening. While Ethan was pretending to be me, I was here at the studio staging it to look like there had been a robbery. It took some work to shut off the security in a way that didn't point

the finger at me. Insurance would never buy it. Everything had to be perfect."

"Why would Ethan agree to it?" I asked. "Art theft
is jail time if you're caught."

"You didn't know my brother," Tyler replied.
"That guy would do anything for money."

I recalled the story Kierra told us about the twins'
mother and my heart pitter-pattered. How could
anyone betray their family for cash? My eyes
narrowed on the monster with the gun. How could
anyone kill for it?

Tilting his body to shield us better, Joe asked,
"How did your brother end up dead?"

"As I said," Tyler said with a shrug. "My brother
would do anything for money. He tried to blackmail
me to give him a bigger cut; said he was taking a lot of
risk to help me so I owed him. I tried to explain that I
had debts to pay off, even reminded him of the all the
times I bailed him out over the years." His eyes flicked
to Kierra. "I didn't tell you because I didn't want you
to worry."

"I'd be less worried if you put the gun away."

"Likewise," Stella agreed.

What the ghost was worried about, I had no idea.
Not like she could die. Again.

Tyler didn't take the bait and only raised his arm

higher. I accidentally stepped forward, and he shoved it further out, training it on my chest. "Don't move."

"Or what, Tyler?" Kierra asked. "You'll shoot her? Kill her the same way you killed Ethan? I don't know who you are."

"What happened to Ethan was an accident!" he screamed. The gun waved, and I almost peed myself as it swung around the room. "He came at me. All I did was fight back. I didn't want to kill him. But then..."

"Then he was already dead, and you saw your way out," Joe finished for him.

Tyler nodded. There was a glimmer in his eyes I hadn't seen before, one that made me realize Tyler was not going to let any of us leave here tonight. Kierra whimpered next to me, her fingers tightening on my arm. I placed a hand on hers and squeezed in reassurance, even though all my bravery had evaporated.

The next few things happened so quickly I couldn't tell one from the other. Standing in the middle of the hallway, Tyler's trigger finger clicked, and a shot rang out. My body was pushed to the side. I landed on top of Kierra, knocking both our breaths out of our lungs. Legs twisting, I turned around to find Joe, only to see him punch Tyler in the chest hard enough to send him barreling backward. The art collector's shoulders smashed into the front door. The hinges rattled under his weight.

With Joe distracted, Tyler took his chance to shoot again. This time, it was me who acted on impulse. While Kierra was distracted beneath me, I pulled out my magic and zapped Tyler's gun hand with electricity so hot it singed his skin. He yelped, the gun clattering from his grip and sliding on the floor toward Joe. My boyfriend lunged for the weapon, securing it before Tyler had a chance to fight back.

That was around the time the cops finally broke inside. The door pulled open, Tyler falling backward as it did. There were so many guns on him, I had trouble counting.

What I could easily count were the people who remained alive and breathing. All three of us by some miracle. Well, us and Stella Rutherford, who was pretending to kick Tyler's butt as the police slapped cuffs on his wrists.

A hand stretched out toward me and I took it, letting Joe pull me up before he helped Kierra. I shook off the remaining sparks of magic from my fingers and shoved them into the pockets of my coat. My shoulders slumped.

It was finally over.

CHAPTER 18

"**M**om! Hurry!"

I raced to the kitchen, my feet sliding the last few steps, hip knocking into the oven. My hands reached for the oven handle and I yanked it open with such force I nearly took it off the hinges. Because the oven was old, not because I was somehow stronger now. Waving a tea towel in the air, I slipped on an oven mitt and pulled out the baking tray inside. My lungs expanded.

Sliding in beside me, my mother chuckled in surprise. "We finally did it."

"Don't you mean I finally did it?"

Mom and I turned together in a perfect spin, our annoyed expressions a mirror of each other. At the counter, Joe was putting the finishing touches on the Gingerbread houses he baked this morning, his hand stretched out for the final batch.

I put the tray next to him. "Well, we made the icing."

"That you did," Joe said. He dunked his finger in the bowl and tapped my nose with it. A dot of cream icing left on the tip. "And it is delicious."

"Someone please shoot us before he licks it off her."

I wiped my nose with a towel, rolled my eyes, and looked at my familiar. "Too soon for those jokes, Stella," I scolded.

The moment the police gave us the go ahead, we packed our bags and raced to Orchard Hollow. With Tyler behind bars and Andrew Well's name cleared, we were allowed to step outside the bounds of the city, just in time for Mom's epic Christmas dinner. The cops assured us that because of the nature of the crime —their big mess up, that was—it would be some time until we would need to return to testify. If ever. According to Joe's buddies, the case against Tyler was done and shut.

The horrible son of a latte admitted his guilt to us in the studio and since Kierra was sticking around to testify as well, Joe doubted they'd bring us in.

I decided not to dwell on it. It was lovely to be home.

Breaking off a piece of cookie from the discarded pile, I chased it with a sip of Eggnog Cappuccino and looked into the living room where Brian stood stoking the fire. Behind him, two tiny raccoon feet protruded from under the couch, stretching out to get closer to the heat emerging from the flames. It was great to see that Harry Houdini had not changed in the short time we'd been away.

Always a trouble maker.

I nudged Joe with my elbow, tipping my head toward the werewolf by the fireplace. "How's he doing?"

"Surprisingly well," Joe answered. "Inviting him tonight was sweet. I think it's helping him take his mind off things. And he's off to see his girls tomorrow, so I know he's excited about that."

I bristled. "Poor Brian. It's one thing to think that your friend died but quite another to find out he was a killer that faked his own death."

"He'll be all right. He's a tough cookie."

"Speaking of cookies..."

My mother's arm snaked around me to steal a piece of broken cookie off the plate. I tried to smack her away but wasn't quick enough and she managed to steal a second piece, which she tucked into her apron.

I was certain she would feed it to the raccoon later, despite my insistence that we put Harry on a healthier diet.

Laughing, I drank my cappuccino and watched Joe work his decorating magic on the dessert. "We should head out soon," I said, noting the late hour. "Everyone will be at Bean Me Up soon." I looked at Mom over my shoulder. "Still can't believe you called half the town over."

"Darling, it's the holidays," she said. "I had to. Especially after everyone on the street stepped up to help when you abandoned me to go solve a murder. As always."

I couldn't even get mad at her. Mom wasn't exaggerating, as she often tended to do. When it became apparent to her that she was in over her head and I was stuck in the city indefinitely, she called every person she knew personally to lend a hand. Every shop on Cliff Row took turns helping her run the place. Some made drinks, others baked muffins at home for us to offer the tourists piling in hour after hour. Cilia even let us borrow a few of the hotel staff from across the street to assist Mom with rush hour traffic.

It was a holiday miracle.

"I'm sorry you had to deal with the cafe," I said, my cheeks warm. "I promise to never leave you like that again."

My mother wrapped an arm around me and pulled me in. Her long silk scarf brushed against my cheek, the scent of her lavender perfume wafting over us. "I'm happy to help, honey. Truly."

She brought two fingers to her lips and let out a loud whistle. At the sound, the tiny feet under the couch wiggled and a big raccoon head popped out from the other side. Harry wiggled his chubby body until he was standing on his hind legs, his paws outstretched. With a swift twirl of the wrist, Mom sent the cookie she grabbed before, flying across the room, right into the raccoon's grubby fingers. Greedily, Harry crammed the cookie into his mouth, puffed out his cheeks, and ducked back underneath the couch.

"Well, I'll be," Stella breathed out. "She tamed the beast."

With a chuckle, I helped Joe pack up the Gingerbread houses to bring them to the car. As we stepped outside, I turned around to see the full gravity of the farmhouse. Above the covered porch, snow piled in big fluffy clouds. Beneath it, the lights we hung twinkled in a myriad of colors, each one reflecting off the snow in a glowing sparkle. Under them, a mistletoe Joe hung swayed in the wind, reminding me to make good use of it later. Smoke rose from the chimney and the frosted windows lent a charm to the place that made my heart melt.

This was what the holidays were all about.

"I know I can't freeze to death, Piper," Stella yelled out from inside Joe's truck. "But I can still die of boredom. Can we go, please?"

I smiled. Turning my back on the farmhouse, I walked down the snowy path to the cars parked in the driveway and climbed in, nestling close to Mom while Brian took the passenger seat. The truck whirred to life and Joe pulled us out of the driveway slow enough for me to glimpse one last view of the house. My eyes landed on the lit up Christmas tree in the living room.

What a perfect day it was! It was nice to know that for once, even a murder couldn't spoil the holiday spirit.

Talk about a Christmas to remember.

EGGNOG CAPPUCCINO

Ingredients:

· 2 cups milk (skim is best for better froth)
· 3.5 tablespoons sugar
· 1 teaspoon vanilla extract
· 2 eggs (beaten)
· Nutmeg (to taste)
· 2 shots of espresso
· Milk frother

Instructions:

1. Blend together the milk, sugar, eggs, vanilla, and nutmeg.
2. Use a frother to get the mixture to be as light and foamy as possible.

3. Pour the espresso into the eggnog mixture.

4. Sprinkle extra nutmeg to the foam.

5. Enjoy!

ABOUT THE AUTHOR

A.N. Sage is a bestselling, award-winning author of mystery and fantasy novels. She has spent most of her life waiting to meet a witch, vampire, or at least get haunted by a ghost. In between failed seances and many questionable outfit choices, she has developed a keen eye for the extra-ordinary.

A.N. spends her free time reading and binge-watching television shows in her pajamas. Currently, she resides in Toronto, Canada with her husband who is not a creature of the night and their daughter who just might be.

A.N. Sage is a Scorpio and a massive advocate of leggings for pants.

For more books and updates:
www.ansage.ca

Connect on social media:
Facebook Group:

facebook.com/groups/945090619339423/

Instagram:

instagram.com/a.n.sage/

TikTok:

tiktok.com/@ansagewrites

YouTube:

youtube.com/c/ANSageWrites